P9-CDU-433

SHARPSHOOTER

VIETNAM

BOOK TWO

SHARPSHOOTER

CHRIS LYNCH

SCHOLASTIC PRESS ★ NEW YORK

All rights reserved. Published by Scholastic Press,
an imprint of Scholastic Inc., *Publishers since 1920.*
SCHOLASTIC, SCHOLASTIC PRESS, and associated
logos are trademarks and/or registered trademarks of Scholastic Inc.

Library of Congress
Cataloging-in-Publication Data
Available

ISBN 978-0-545-27026-7

10 9 8 7 6 5 4 3 2   12 13 14 15 16
Printed in the U.S.A.   23
First edition, April 2012

The text type was set in Sabon MT.
Book design by Christopher Stengel

PART ONE

CHAPTER ONE

Sometimes Things
Gotta Be Broken

My pal Morris is a top-shelf guy, but man, enough already with the pledges. If the boy had a motto it would be, *A pledge for everything, and everything in a pledge.*

Since we were kids, the four of us — myself, Morris, Rudi, and Beck — have been signing up to one solemn oath after another: to say we would not ever compete for the same girl, that we would back each other up in any hopeless, stupid endeavor, and that our four lunches were basically joint property. It's dangerously close to communism the way we do this, but because they're such great friends I make the necessary effort to overlook it.

The big pledge, though, is going to be the test.

Morris started getting these nightmares, on account of the nightly news. (Thanks a lot for that, Mr. Walter Cronkite.) The Vietnam War is coming over loud and clear and blood-red every night, and it's scaring the ever-loving out of our sweet, sensitive Morris. Practically every day he comes to school with tales from the

Technicolor horror of his subconscious — tales that always end with the grisly death of the four of us in Vietnam.

But so what?

"Everybody's got to do their bit, Morris, when the call comes," I say as we change into our red gym shorts and gray T-shirts. We have gym class together in this final semester of our whole school lives.

"No," he says, grimly and quite seriously.

"No?" I respond. "No? How do you figure no?"

"Listen, Ivan, man," he says, "I can't live with it. Okay? I can't live with the idea of us, of *you*" — in a highly uncharacteristic gesture he pokes me hard in the chest — "of any of us, going all the way over there to be slaughtered. The dead part will be horrible enough, but the right-now of it is, I swear, eating me alive."

I finish tying my sneakers, get up off the bench in front of my locker, and stare down at him. "So," I say, "bump yourself off now and eliminate the unbearable suspense."

"Ivan," he says, scrambling after me as I head for the gym. He hasn't even had time to do up his laces. "I'm not joking. We have to talk about this."

"No," I say, "we don't." I am longing for the relentless, bouncing, echoey sound of the cold brick-wall gym full of nut jobs dribbling and hooting and implying disgusting things about one another's mothers.

As I get to the door, he catches up and, in another unusual maneuver, grabs the waistband of my shorts hard with both hands, yanking me to a halt. I stand there, motionless, refusing to turn.

"Ivan?" he says, and he sounds so pathetic I am panicked somebody will hear us together and I will be lame by association.

I sigh. "I detect the stench of a pact coming on, Morris."

"You cannot join up," he says.

I sigh a little more dramatically. You see, I am a military man. My dad is a military man — he rode with Patton in North Africa, saved the world and all that, and had a fine time doing it. I am a fighter. I was born to fight. I like to fight, as long as it is a good and proper, righteous fight.

This pact is about me. Rudi, Beck, and Morris are in no danger of putting themselves forward for duty. But Morris is asking something big of me here, and he well knows it.

And I know there is nothing in the world I could not ask of him. That's the thing. The rat.

"What if I get drafted?" I ask.

The pause indicates he has not even dared to consider this. But he responds true to form.

"Then I'll join. If any one of us gets drafted, I'm joining."

I laugh out loud at him. I laugh at the notion of Morris in any kind of military situation. And I laugh at the drop-dead certainty of his offer.

"You don't have to do that," I say.

"Yes," he says, "I do."

Of course he does. He is Morris. Truer and bluer do not exist in nature.

I push open the door into the bouncing gym madness and Morris steps up next to me.

Then *boom*, he takes a ball right in the kisser and drops to the floor like a dead man.

I look down at him as he attempts to shake his faculties back to life.

"How many?" I ask, holding up four fingers.

"Four," he says. "But that doesn't prove anything because you always hold up four."

"Good answer," I say, offering him a grin but not a hand up. I am too busy for that as I spin and stomp away.

I have to go polish the gym floor with somebody's face.

It wasn't even a dodge ball. That was a basketball, so no, this cannot be allowed to stand.

This early, and already I am in for a fight and detention.

Jeez, Morris, you and your pledges.

CHAPTER TWO

Tribal

If there is anybody built to fight more than me, it's my father. He claims a genetic link to every legendary legion history has ever produced. Spartans, Huns, Vikings — he swears he's got their blood in him. Romans, Ottomans, Prussians — there is not an empire that has passed over the earth without also, passing through Dad's bloodline somewhere along the way.

Nothing makes him prouder, though, than his American Indian heritage, which he swears is Sioux despite the fact that his father always insisted it was the less famous, less feisty Narragansett tribe. No matter.

"The *right* fight," he says, pointing his gnarled tree-root of a finger at me. To get the fingertip to point at the spot between my eyes, he has to aim somewhere around my right jaw muscle. He got that condition in North Africa, fighting shoulder to shoulder with General Patton. That was a famously —

"Right fight, Ivan."

"I recognize one when I see one, Dad," I say.

The two of us are doing something we do a lot: watching the news together. We watch it the same way some folks watch sports. Edge of our seats, much gesturing, much commentary. Mom can't watch these days. Because of the war. But my younger brother, Caesar, is with us, half playing, half serious, totally working on imitating my father — his postures, words, ideas.

He could do a lot worse, Caesar, than to imitate the old man.

He's only thirteen, though, so he's got a good while to practice.

The two of them are eating their dinner in front of the TV, pointing sweet late-summer corn on the cobs at the scenes of wild Vietnam action.

"That is a right fight, Dad," Caesar says.

"Any fight your country is in is a right fight, son," Dad says.

Dad claims his famous martial bloodline was flowing on *both* sides of the battle of the Little Bighorn. He says, relative or not, General George got what he had coming to him.

"When do you go, Ivan?" Caesar asks me.

Rats.

He hasn't even bothered to ask me *if* I'm going. That's who we are in this family. We are so natural and comfortable with the idea of warfare that my little brother can be eating and watching bloodshed on TV at the very same time as wondering casually when I'm going to throw myself on the spit, too. He could just as easily be asking me to go shoot baskets at the Y down the street.

So it's okay to be casual about marching off to war, but it sure ain't okay to be casual about not marching.

The subject of the pledge has come up only once in the two weeks since I committed myself to not committing myself. That conversation went well — my father mocked me so mercilessly that I pretended it was all a joke.

Dad thought it was the stupidest thing he ever heard.

I kind of feel that way myself, which makes this situation even worse.

They are eating and I am not because I am, in fact, going out to meet Morris and the guys up on Peters Hill at the Arboretum, like we do on a Thursday night. I bring the drinks, Morris brings Fontaine's amazing boneless fried chicken, Beck freaks me out by bringing baked goods *that he makes himself*, and Rudi shocks everyone by bringing himself, not getting run over, and possibly remembering some more drinks.

"I don't know, Caesar," I say, standing from my chair, pointing at him like I am making an appointment to discuss the matter in greater detail at a later date.

Dad takes a bite of pork chop, looks at me with a squint, and gives me a very similar, more loaded point with his crooked finger.

"I know, Dad," I say, backing out of the room, calling good-bye to Mom in the kitchen, and hustling myself out of harm's way and into the night.

I am far more afraid of telling my father than facing any Vietcong or North Vietnamese Army.

In fact, I am *itching* to face those guys. I'm feeling a little cheated, not going.

I stop at the store on the way up to the Arboretum. I pass two stores before I stop at the one I stop at, Garcia's, because Garcia's is the one that carries Moxie. Moxie is the world's finest drink. It started out as a medicine, and I am convinced it gives me strength. On the long list of things that make America great, Moxie comes in around five or six. And because apparently Moxie is a thing that is largely unappreciated outside of New England, that is another good reason why New England is right up there. And Garcia's, too, since they have the good taste to carry Moxie, as well as being the only place around where you can get batteries on Christmas Day if you get a present that needs them.

It is a good long hike from my house up to Peters Hill, but I don't mind at all. I like a good long hike.

I am thinking about exactly that as I hike along. *I like a good long hike.*

Something's got to give.

I am supposed to bring a full six-pack, but Moxie helps me think. I pop open a can, put the pull tab on my pinkie like jewelry, and I hike and I think.

Two things are right here, but they are in opposition.

One: You cannot break a pledge. No man worth spit ever breaks a pledge. Your word has got to be your word.

Two: You cannot shirk your duty when you know your duty.

Rats.

I haven't walked a half mile before I open a second drink. But it's working. I can feel it. I am thinking more clearly. The evening air, the brisk pace, the magic of Moxie.

It is the lamest pledge we ever made, after all. Certain pledges deserve to be unpledged.

But not broken. That's a violation right there, and violations won't do.

We are going to have to talk about this. We have to come to the negotiating table, and if it means I am responsible for Morris's nightmares going atomic, that may just have to be my burden to bear.

As I march up the steep hill to where the guys are, I don't even feel the gradient. It is as if I am walking level or downhill, even. I am full of energy and purpose and rightness. I have to sort out this pledge thing and get it behind us and get the enemy in front of us. Well, in front of me, at least. The rest of these tadpoles can do what they want with the next four years.

I see Beck and Morris as I approach, before they see me. They are sitting on the granite slab that acts as a bench for looking out at the Boston skyline. They look awfully cute, sitting there side by side like they're on a date or something, until eventually Beck has the sense to put Morris in a headlock. Their version of fighting. I bet the Vietcong are pretty relieved these guys are staying home.

"Hey, is this what happens when I show up late?" I ask.

They turn to face me, and I am prepared to launch right into my case for joining the Army.

But I see their faces, and I flinch. Stupid Morris and his stupid nightmares. This should be easier.

"Ugh," Morris says, "again with the Moxie? That stuff tastes like carbonated tires."

The ungrateful little wart, I should tell him right now. I should tell him I signed up for the Army and while I was at it I volunteered him, too.

But I have too much self-discipline for that. So I tell him another necessary truth instead.

"Quiet. Nobody needs Moxie more than you do."

"You were supposed to bring a full six," Beck says.

I'm supposed *to be joining the Army,* I say in my head.

"Yeah, well, I mugged myself on the way over," is what I say out loud. "I put up a brave fight, though. Where's Bozo, anyway?"

"Not here yet," Morris says. The two of them have plucked drinks off the rack I brought. It feels like a hostage exchange when I go for the chicken. Fontaine's boneless fried chicken is the kind of thing you defend your country for, and I cannot be shy about going for it. I reach into the bucket and pull out an uncivilized fistful. Then I walk a few feet away to plunk down on a boulder and gather myself, my thoughts, and my words, and I wait for Rudi to complete the picture. When he does, I gotta talk. I tear into the chicken and hardly even chew it. I look like a caveman on my rock. I don't care.

"There he is," Morris says after only a minute. Rudi is coming, straight up the steep and grassy side of Peters Hill, where the Boston skyline is floating above the trees and high above the boy himself. It is the hard way up.

If there is a hard way to anything, Rudi takes it. Unintentionally.

I laugh to myself, thinking that. Then I stop laughing.

This is insane that I feel like this. This is stupid. Every cell in my body knows I want to go to Vietnam, and every cell knows I should go.

And then I think about these guys. These three jamokes have been just *right there* in every piece of my life for as long as I've been taking notice. Dumb as they can be, and much as I would hate to admit it out loud, these pledges mean something. They have always meant something. They were always the cement that made us one structure rather than the modules we were otherwise. I mean, in what universe would Morris and I be part of an unbreakable *thing*? Or Rudi and Beck? This universe. Ours.

But there comes a time.

Guys gotta grow up.

Things gotta be broken.

"What's that he's carrying?" Beck asks.

Rudi is nearing the top, flapping and panting as he approaches. Then he stands there in front of us for a few seconds. He sticks a sheet of paper in front of Beck's face.

"Does this mean what I think it means?" Rudi whimpers. "Tell me what it means, Beck, man. You're smart, I'm stupid. Tell me I got it wrong, and it doesn't mean what I think."

Beck starts reading, and from the sinking look on his face it doesn't take long for the meaning to come clear — to me, anyway.

I know the wording. I think my family once had napkins with this printed on them.

" 'You are hereby directed to present yourself for Armed Forces Physical Examination . . . ' " I recite.

I had completely forgotten. Although Rudi graduated with us, he is a year older because of having gotten kept back in fourth grade. That means he is nineteen. That means once he performed the miracle of graduating high school with the rest of us, he became eligible for the draft.

It's Moxie time.

I pop my third Moxie, decorate a third finger with a metal pull tab, and watch them try to put it all together.

"Have a brownie, pal," Beck says to Rudi. Rudi takes the brownie. He begins crying. He fits himself in on the rock between Morris and Beck.

I grow impatient watching the three of them poring over the paper like a bunch of overgrown six-year-olds trying to read along to a hymn sheet. And trying to make it say something other than what it says.

I get up and step right over to them. "What?" I say, then snatch the notice right out of Beck's hands.

I'm reading the words, and checking the details, and

getting the picture the others do not want to get. I feel my hips start to shimmy. I feel myself smiling. I don't want anybody to be upset, really I don't. But this is right. The other thing was wrong. What is happening should be happening and I could not pretend to be unhappy about this rightness if I tried.

When it comes down to it, I don't know if I was going to be able to break my pledge. I like to think I would have done it.

But I like better that I didn't have to.

I dance with the sheet, dance with Rudi's notice to report. I dance it to the edge of the hill, with my boys behind me and my Boston all in front of me. I spin back to the guys, then back again toward the skyline, with my hands in the air.

"We . . . are . . . goin' . . . to . . . *Nam*, boys!" I shout.

I slam that notice onto the ground in celebration, then I rush up to Rudi, thanking him, congratulating him.

He shakes back. Tries smiling. Does more crying. His face, I see now, looks like it's being pulled by tiny wires in all different directions.

Oh. I'd have known this if I were thinking. I should have known this is how he'd feel. But oh.

"Rudi, buddy, you're gonna be fine," I say, grabbing him by the shoulders. "You're gonna be more than fine. You're gonna be a man. And you're gonna be a hero."

Morris does his version of being helpful. "Or maybe he'll fail his physical," he says.

"This boy ain't failing nothin'," I say, being more helpful, though less truthful.

Because, truth is, our man Rudi could fail the task of falling flat on his face, if falling flat on his face was called for. And if you're being shot at it could well be called for. He's already failed at *receiving* his notice for his physical, as he has arrived here this evening with honest-to-goodness pee staining the front of him.

Beck jumps away from him. "Jeez, Rudi, you didn't even change your pants?"

"I came running. I had to. Had to see you guys . . ."

I decide in this situation the best thing to do is to mock and ridicule Rudi. So that everything seems normal.

"The Rudi peed his pants *dance*," I sing, adding a crisp sorta conga dance thing. "The Rudi peed his pants . . ."

But as I scramble my brain for rhymes to keep this going, I stumble on *peed* and *need*. He rushed here soaking wet because in his hour of need, his need was us.

And so I cut the dance, and the song, and for a second there I almost give in to getting all emotional.

But we all need some thing or other. That's just how it goes. And this is how this goes.

"Army, baby. The armored cavalry, just like my old man," I say when Morris has the nerve to question my happiness. "Wait 'til I tell my dad. He always thought Morris's pledge was an ol' nancy pledge anyway." Or he would have if he believed it was anything but a joke. "No offense, Morris."

"Of course not," he says.

"Now we got a real pledge, boys," I say. "A *man's* pledge."

I pick up Rudi's notice off the ground and bring it to him. I present it, formal-like, then give him a perfect sharp salute that would make my father proud.

Rudi is sniffling like a kid when he does his best to answer in kind. It's not half bad, though wiping tears with his free hand compromises it a little bit.

The four of us spend a few seconds looking out at the Boston skyline, and it feels like a big ol' see-ya-later to the town. Then we turn to each other and lean into a spontaneous huddle, like a football huddle, like we are planning out the big play before we go out there and mow 'em down.

Can't wait to talk to my dad now.

CHAPTER THREE

Paragon

I passed my physical," Rudi says, mixing pride and joylessness into a whole new emotion.

"I know, man. Congratulations."

"Thanks," he says.

We are walking on Nantasket Beach, first of July, perfect summer day, perfect. The waves are crashing, the sun is scorching. The beach is mobbed, and the sounds of screeching kids in the sand and screeching seagulls in the air are identical. We are just passing into the atmosphere of Carousel Kitchen, in the shadow of the roller coaster, where the scent of the ocean collides with the scent of fried clams to slaughter every other scent into oblivion.

"They probably didn't even bother *giving* you a physical," Rudi says, accusingly.

"Well, yeah, they did," I say. "You want some clams if I'm buyin'?"

"Of course I'm wantin' if you're buyin'. So what'd you score, like, a million?"

"You don't get points, dumbo," Caesar says, jumping on Rudi's back and giving his skull machine-gun noogies.

"I passed," I say as we head to the clam stand.

Caesar hops down off Rudi's back as we wait to order. They do a little bit of fake boxing while I play the role of authority. I could almost be the father here, but the sizes don't work. Rudi is almost my height, though not built as big. Caesar is shorter than us by four or five inches yet, though you might still guess he was the older of my two sons.

Everyone everywhere is older than Rudi.

We take our three boxes of clams to the seawall, to eat and watch the tide, to go forward and back and forward in our heads.

"You excited about going, Rudi?" Caesar asks.

"No, sir," Rudi says, and stuffs three fat clams in his mouth like he's trying to gag himself.

"What?" Caesar says. He is his father's son, his grandfather's grandson and all that, so he has to work to understand the mindset.

"Rudi's a lover, not a fighter," I tell Caesar as three girls in bathing suits walk past and smile at us.

"Can't you be both?" Caesar asks.

"Can I be *either*?" Rudi asks, staring at the girls like they just emerged out of the sea with tentacles sprouting out of their heads.

I am sitting between the two of them, on the wall, facing out to sea. The park, with the roller coaster, the screaming, the mad rides and games and crazy mental fun, is blowing hot breath at our backs. Waves are crashing ahead of us, but it's the calm of the ocean farther out that catches my attention and holds it.

What *is* going to happen to him?

"I *said*" — Rudi is elbowing me — "can I have some of your drink?"

"No. Get your own drink. You know I don't like sharing drinks."

"So how come you didn't buy drinks for us? You bought the clams. Doesn't it make sense to buy drinks to go with the clams?"

Caesar eats silently. He knows better. Rudi never, ever does.

"Fried clams make you really thirsty, Ivan. You know that. I know you know that because you bought *yourself* a drink, so —"

I smack him. I turn, go cross-eyed, and smack Rudi right across the back of the head, knocking him off the wall and into the sand six or so feet below.

Caesar laughs so hard I believe I detect a clam oozing its way out his nose. Rudi manages to hit the beach and still keep his clam box upright.

"Hey," he snaps up at me. He scoops up a fried clam that managed to pop up and escape during the tumble.

"Give it to the gulls, man," I say wearily, because I know better but have to try anyway.

"It's fine, it's fine," Rudi says, blowing on the thing like the Big Bad Wolf. "It came from the sand in the first place, didn't it, when it was still alive?"

I can feel it in my own mouth, the grains of sand grinding and crunching in Rudi's teeth before he spits it out.

Caesar and I laugh and fall over each other. Then Caesar holds out a clam, which Rudi jumps up and snags like he is in fact a seagull.

"There," Caesar says. "So you didn't lose out in the end."

Rudi nods, very serious about the transaction and the rightness of it.

Then he looks up at me, a kind of begging face I don't want to see.

"Don't start," I say, putting out a hand to pull him back up.

"How could you really want to go to Vietnam, Ivan?" he asks as he gets to the top of the wall.

I shrug, and the three of us start walking in the direction of the Paragon Park amusements. "I'm a fighting man," I say. "Fighting men fight when they are called to do so."

"Fight people around here, then," he says, and means it.

The rides of Paragon Park are legendary, especially the roller coaster, the Giant Coaster. We have come here a few times each summer since we were old enough to make it down to Nantasket without parental supervision. We used to come *with* parental supervision, but it's not at all the same.

"It's not the same, Rudi," I say. "Even you know that."

"I know," he says, and then he realizes what is happening. "I also know I will not be going on that thing." He points his last floppy fried clam up at the Giant Coaster.

"You have to be kidding," Caesar says. Caesar never came to Nantasket with us all those times. He was just a kid. Now with him being thirteen and me shipping out, this felt like one of those things I needed to get around to.

My brother is jumping up and walking backward and taunting Rudi like Muhammad Ali. "You goin', Rudi. You goin', you goin' *up*." He gestures up at the towering and thundering wooden roller coaster that sounds like it's going to pull itself to pieces at every turn. And there are a lot of turns.

It still gives me butterflies.

Every time I come here I feel the same rush. But there's more to it now. Because we have the coaster, which is ferocious, but then we have all the past stuff, the history. All the times we have taken the ride, stood up when we shouldn't have. The girls we screamed at down on the ground to wait for us who were never there when we got down. The older guys we threw french fries at — who *always* seemed to be there when we got down. And the view of the sea, how you could almost taste the water, and the weird way the ocean salt and the shake and slam of the ride somehow made you need a hot dog.

Beck always pretended to be bored with the thrill ride but thrilled with the stars and clouds. Morris never pretended he was brave but never once chickened out, even when he already had a shirt spotted here and there with his own spittle.

And Rudi.

"Stop laughing!" he shouts at me now, like he shouted at me then.

"You have to go on there this time," I say, laughing and punching the air around his head.

"He's never gone on?" Caesar says, excited as a terrier pup. "Never, ever?"

"Not quite exactly true," I say.

"I have so gone on," Rudi insists.

I laugh more.

"Stop laughing," he says.

"Did he go on or not?" Caesar asks, slapping my arm.

"I did!"

"He did, he did. He just didn't see anything. He suddenly turned into this circus contortionist, just at the point where the coaster slows right down. And *ker-klink, ker-klink* . . ."

"Stop it, Ivan," Rudi says, and raises his hand to his brow like he's shading from the sun. "That's what got me the first time."

"I know. That slow death of the sound and the stop-start and the yanking of the chain as you get pulled up to the highest point of the coaster and it seems like it's stalled . . ."

"I love that," says Caesar.

"Right," I say. "And suddenly this guy becomes Gumby, bends himself every which way, with me laughing and pulling at him until he squirms himself right down into the foot well of the coaster car, I mean right down there like a dog, and he stays there, screaming and howling every single second of the way. People down on the ground, people all the way out on the beach, even, could hear Rudi's screaming above all the other screaming. There were people pointing, cheering. I mean, it's a big amusement park, for cryin' out loud, it's almost impossible to make a spectacle of yourself, right? But he's screamin' and wailin' . . ."

"Until the end," he says apologetically.

"Until the end," I say scoldingly.

We are just about to the entrance to the rides area. Above us, and around us, the world is having a shouty, sweaty, fantastic day at the park.

"What did you do to my shoes, Rudi? Hmmmm?" I wag my finger. "What did you do to Daddy's shoes, bad dog, to make all the people laugh?"

"I am really, really sorry for that, Ivan," he says, still apologizing years later as if my shoes were still mucky. "I didn't mean it. See, I was very scared . . ."

Here is the thing I get about Rudi that makes all the difference. And it's the thing I badly hope the North Vietnamese get about him while he is over there visiting their part of the world: Even when he has just done something to make you want to kill him, you look in his eyes and it makes you want to hug him.

I hope they get that. I don't really expect them to, though.

Mostly, I don't hug him, but I don't blow his head off, either.

"You can make it up to me," I say, taking him by the arm and leading him to the ticket line.

"Ivan, no," he says. "No, I can't."

He is covering his ears like we are in the middle of an air raid. Caesar has gone around the other side of him, and it looks as if we are hauling the Cowardly Lion to face the Wizard of Oz.

"We'll discuss it," I say. It is only the entrance to the

park itself he has to face yet. All the individual rides can be confronted on a horror-by-horror basis.

"We're not going on any of those baby rides on Rudi's list, are we, Ivan?"

"Of course not," I say. It's okay to be a little less gentle with Rudi now that he's got a slice of sausage pizza in one hand and a box of taffy in the other. And watching through the window at Lehange's as the big taffy-pulling machine turns over and over has enough of a soothing effect that Rudi agrees to some rides.

Very particular rides.

"There were no baby rides on my list."

"Um, Carousel? Um, Teacups?"

"Right," Rudi says, as if he is now making his big redemption move. He dashes to where the line is empty for the Kooky Kastle.

Caesar looks at me, and I smile. It is hardly any-thing death defying, but I have always had a soft spot for the Kastle. It is a not-very-spooky train ride in the dark through this castlelike structure. It's less fun than the Congo Cruise, which is a sort of darkened boat ride through a big head. Most of the thrills and chills on that are created by passengers rocking the boat, throw-ing stuff in the water, throwing people in the water, grabbing the cave walls so that the boat stops and the fumes from the fetid water nearly wipe out all the passengers. That sort of thing. Not at all Rudi's cup of sludge.

The Kastle, though, should be okay. We come up behind Rudi, who bounces from foot to foot with either anticipation or nerves. They both tend to look the same on Rudi.

The ride is a continuous procession of unconnected cars, each holding no more than two passengers.

"Now, this is more like it, huh, Rude," I say, smacking his leg so hard the echo off the walls sounds like one of the sound effects.

"Yeah," he says, but even with this modest ride, even with this, I sense the tremor inside him.

Frankenstein begins chasing an innocent lady around in a circle. She is out of his reach by about three feet. He has been that close for many years.

"Relax, lady," I call out. "I happen to know he runs exactly as fast as you do."

Rudi says nothing. I see his hands tightly squeezing his knees, and his head is down. Bats on elastic strings flutter past.

He's being so weird I'm actually getting creeped out in the Kooky Kastle for the first time since I was about six.

"Rudi, what the —"

"I'm thinking about not going!" he shouts, the words bouncing and bending around all the walls of the ride.

I wait for them to settle. A mummy comes popping out of a coffin and I automatically punch the face, cracking it and bruising my hand.

"Not going where?" I ask.

"You know where."

"Help me out."

"You help *me* out, Ivan. That's the way it's supposed to work, right? *Something* needs to work the way it's supposed to work right now."

I am staring at the side of his head as we go in and out of shadow and low light. Recorded howls and shrieks from overhead speakers barely register.

"Not going where, Rudi?"

"Never mind," he says, nutty enough to be a part of the Kooky Kastle staff. "Never mind, never mind, never mind."

"Marines? Not going to the Marines?"

"Marines isn't a place, stupid," he says, foolishly.

"Hey, wiseguy," I say, low in his ear, "if you recall, you weren't *asked* to go anywhere."

"Vietnam. Aw, Ivan, even when I say the word . . . aw, Ivan . . . remember what I did to your shoes? I feel like I'm going to do it again, to everybody's shoes in the world."

I have looked away from him now, straight ahead as the ride winds down, then away in the opposite direction. I feel him breathing, right on my neck in terrified little puffs.

This would be that moment where you want to kill him but you can't because you look in his eyes and he's all Rudi on you and you just can't kill him.

So I won't look at his Rudi eyes.

Because I'm afraid I might see it different now.

The ride comes to an end when this dummy zombie drops down out of the ceiling above and rocket blasts of air shoot you from left and right before the car punches through the doors and back out into the shock of the sunlight.

Caesar is standing, laughing, on the platform as we pull up.

"Let's go again," Caesar says, angling back toward the entrance as if we have already decided. "I just nearly pulled the head off that Dracula guy, and I bet I can get him this time."

"You go," I say. "We'll wait here."

"Chicken?"

"Yes, Caesar, chicken," I growl. "Go!"

He is gone.

There is a bench where old people and the lame sit to wait for more robust parkgoers to come off the ride. We sit there.

"You don't have a choice," I say. I am trying to hold back my disgust, just because he is Rudi. I honestly don't know if I can hold it for long, though. "What would you do?"

"Run," he says, as if he has actually put thought into this.

I can feel my voice drop, though I don't do it on purpose.

"Say again?"

"No," he says, sliding down the bench away from me.

"Have I told you about my father and General Patton?" I say.

"Please don't slap me, Ivan."

I stare out at the ocean. I listen to the sounds of people having the whole world of fun right here at Paragon Park, exactly like we would have been doing if this was last year and we were still kids in school.

"You're thinking of running."

"I am thinking of running."

I can hear my brother's great big goofy kid laugh from here. I would know it from anywhere in the world, and I figure he's about halfway through the Kastle and carrying a plastic Dracula's head.

"All right then, Rudi, man. So why tell me? Huh? You know what I'm gonna say. You know who I am. You and I both know what I'm gonna say. That fool driving the Chevy Impala over there knows what I'm gonna say."

The doors to the Kastle burst open and my brother, cackling, races past, carrying Dracula's head. Running behind him is a chubby park employee Dracula without a plastic head.

"Headless Dracula even knows what I'm gonna say."

"Uh-huh," Rudi agrees.

"You tell Beck you were gonna run?"

"No."

"Morris?"

"No."

"Hunh," I say, and I will confess there is a part of this story that is converting my anger into pride. Just a small part, but it's there. "You'd think you would tell those guys before you'd tell me, wouldn't you? You'd think you'd be in Sweden or someplace before you'd tell me, wouldn't you? Why not tell the other guys, Rudi?"

He stands up, breathes deep — he's trying to come up biggish and strong — and makes his way to stand right in front of me.

"'Cause they would tell me to run."

Of course they would. They're his best friends. They want what is best for him.

"And me?"

"And you . . . wouldn't allow it. You would terrorize me or humiliate me or just plain old beat me, until I did my duty."

Of course I would. I'm his best friend. I want what is best for him.

I stand up and nose-to-nose him. Like a drill sergeant to a raw recruit.

"Where would you like me to start, boy?" I say firmly.

"You can slap me now if you like, sir."

I remain practically touching his nose with mine. But not. I can't fight a smile of . . . something like pride, I guess you'd call it.

Then I pull back and I slap that poor, stupid, trusting, stupid, simple great face with enough pop to make General George S. Patton himself cry.

But does my boy cry?

Of course he does.

"I'm scared, Ivan."

"I know you are."

"But I'm going."

"I know you are."

He remains, tearstained and at attention until finally, he just nods at me.

"The Marine Corps is going to love you, pal, trust me."

"I trust you more than anybody else in the world. So yeah. But they better love me while they can, because I don't expect to be alive very long."

CHAPTER FOUR

Kick the Can

My parents have decided that the best way they can support the war effort right now — since the Army told my dad he is too old to go and he has already given them me — is to fortify the four of us with a going-away dinner that will live on in our muscles and minds and hearts until the day we come back.

I go to Rudi's house to deliver the invitation in person, as his phone appears to be out of order. His phone is out of order more than most people's. He lives on the top floor of a triple-decker near Forest Hills that he shares with his mother and the occasional lodger who takes up the spare bedroom for a few weeks at a time. When I climb all the way up the stairs, the current lodger greets me at the door. He may have a home at the moment, but he smells like he doesn't.

"We are having a big send-off dinner at my house," I say to Rudi as he lies on his bed, examining the GI Joe he has had since he was six.

"Do we have to?" is Rudi's response.

He's not unappreciative. In fact, one time he ate dinner at Beck's house, and he was so grateful they found him outside mowing their lawn at seven o'clock the next morning.

"I'm sorry, Ivan, but The Captain is the most intimidating man on earth. Even if I could make myself go there and sit at his table and everything, I'm sure my throat would never open up enough for me to be able to swallow any food at all. And that would be insulting to your mom. And, jeez, I can't even begin to think about what happens to a person who is disrespectful to The Captain's wife."

His shoulders shiver visibly at the tail end there.

The Captain, obviously, is my father. He rose as high as captain in the Army, and since that's exactly where he is now in the State Police chain, I think Captain is his fair designation all over life. I can see where people might find him intimidating. Doesn't mean he isn't a great man, and a perfectly nice host.

"You can't say no," I say to Rudi. "He'll beat me. I'll show up for the war looking like I've already been there."

I really shouldn't mess with the guy like this. But there are lots of things I shouldn't do.

"Aw," he moans. "Ivan . . . I can't let that happen."

"Of course you can't. So you will be there tomorrow night, and you will eat and not choke, which would ruin everybody else's dinner."

"Fine," he says.

I sit down on the bed, dropping myself right onto his outstretched legs. He doesn't retract them. I grab Joe away from him and do a quick inspection. He is wearing his camouflage outfit, which is not surprising as it is his only outfit. He has the fuzzy hair, too.

"You thinking this is gonna be you?" I ask him.

"Really, I was thinking it was gonna be you," he says, taking the action figure back from me. "*This* is gonna be me." He snaps the man's head off.

"Oh, put that back," I say. "For better or for worse, your head is going to remain right where it is. And tomorrow night, six o'clock, I want to see that head and the rest of you at my house. Don't be late. You can imagine how The Captain feels about punctuality."

"He's in favor of it?"

"Insanely in favor. And since it is my last night in town, I'm kind of serious about it myself, since who knows when I'll see you all again."

"When, or *if*."

I stare at him. "Do I have to commence the slapping again?"

"No, sir. See you at six tomorrow."

I give his legs a good strong bounce as I get up and go.

We will all be gone within a week. I go first, which is only right. Rudi and Morris both ship out three days later, Beck two days after that.

It's starting to feel very real.

I march crisply to the door as soon as the bell rings. When I open up, all three stooges are lined up on the step. Rudi is holding flowers for my mom, Morris has two six-packs of drinks — one Moxie, one orange soda for the sadly misguided — and Beck is cradling a pan of something covered in foil and smelling of molasses.

"Orange soda and home baking, that's the Navy and Air Force for ya," I say.

I lead them into the living room, where The Captain and Mom await. Dad practically leaps off the couch to greet the guys. He's so enthusiastic about this you would think he was greeting guys returning from war rather than diving into it.

"Men," Dad says, stepping up to each guy individually and saluting. "Now normally, it would be you saluting me first, because I outrank you. But we won't stand on ceremony here."

"Whoa, really letting your hair down there, Dad," I say.

There is a two-second silence. Beck laughs. Then I get a clip behind the ear, and everybody laughs.

"Thank you so much," Mom says as she takes the flowers from Rudi. There are visible clumps of root and dirt sticking out of the bottom of the paper. Lord knows where he collected the things, but the arrangement is pretty nice. She gives him a massive squeeze. He looks embarrassed at first but then gives all the way in, not only hugging her back but even laying his head down on her shoulder.

"Shall we head to the dining room?" Dad says.

"Yes, sir, Captain," Beck says. I have always enjoyed Beck's relationship with my father, though it has the slightest suggestion of danger to it. Or maybe *because* it has the slightest suggestion of danger to it. Beck's world, of arts and sciences, of mind over matter, is kind of at odds with my father's take on life. So in a way they intrigue each other as totally foreign species. But at times it seems Beck is sailing critically close to provoking something from the old man. Not advisable.

"Remember," my father says, wagging a playful finger at him before nudging him in the direction of the dining room, "where you're going, you are not always going to be the smartest guy in the room."

Yes he is. But anyway.

"And even if you were," Dad continues, "it probably wouldn't be in your best interest to advertise that fact."

That is advice that sounds a little more helpful.

"I hope he gives *me* advice like that," Rudi whispers to me as we step into the room.

"He will," I say. "I'm sure he'll tell you the exact same thing, man."

"Excellent," Rudi says.

My father has never been one of those tight-lipped veterans who don't like to discuss their wartime experiences. He is immensely proud of what he did in World War II under General Patton. And he should be. There are pictures all over the house, in fact, keeping that experience alive. Photos of Patton, of course, and of scores of the tanks and fighter planes active in North Africa and Europe. General Ike Eisenhower is there, too, in our bathroom, and General Omar Bradley on the upstairs landing. But the art-of-warfare museum thing really reaches its peak in our dining room.

"Wow," Morris says, taking in the scene. Each of the four walls has a different theme. There is an American Revolution wall, a World War I wall, a Civil War wall. And the main attraction, above the sideboard, is Dad's tribute to the Indian Wars of the Old West. Like I said, he sees himself, remarkably, on both sides.

"You like it?" Dad says, beaming. Morris is at the sideboard, leaning right on it to examine the central item. The other guys huddle around so The Captain has to push past them to point out the fine detail of his proudest acquisition, a print of a painting called *Founding Fathers*.

The painting is a two-tiered thing. The lower half is the familiar scene of Mount Rushmore, the lineup same as it ever was: George Washington, Thomas Jefferson, Theodore Roosevelt, and Abraham Lincoln, left to right. The twist, though, is that these founding fathers of America are not hogging the spotlight for themselves the way they're used to. Hovering in a similar formation above them are the faces of four great leaders of the American Indian Nations.

Sitting Bull is there, and Crazy Horse. The other two gents, it's a little embarrassing to say, have never been definitively identified. At least, not in this house.

To be more accurate, I should say that they have in fact been definitively identified by my father on many occasions. Only, the definitive identifications change. Sometimes Red Cloud is up there. Sometimes Cochise, sometimes Geronimo. Their identities seem to have more to do with my dad's current reading material than any serious study into the matter.

"You know we are descended from the Sioux," Dad says to the guys.

"Your father always said Narragansett," Mom says, setting down a big tureen of soup.

"Ach," Dad says. "Narragansett. Who'd they ever fight?"

Dad scowls, then continues his seminar. "We did a family tree a while back. Turns out we are related to every one of those great men. Direct blood relations."

Even I have lost track of how much of it he truly believes. If he said direct *spiritual* relations, rather than blood, he'd be one hundred percent truthful. Dad sees his head right up there with all the founding warriors, there is no doubt of that.

I go to the kitchen with Mom to fetch, while Dad continues his lecture. When we come back in with platters of roast beef, mashed potatoes, buttery green beans with almond slivers, gravy, and corn bread, everybody is seated and waiting.

The scents that fill the room are everything you want your house to smell like. Warm and rich, familiar and friendly. Satisfying and safe.

These are the smells we are going to fight for.

"I don't imagine you'll see the likes of this meal again for some time," Dad says.

"Oh, sure they will," Mom says, slapping his arm. "Don't make such a big deal."

"Would anyone like to say grace?" Dad asks.

Beck shoots me a look like he might laugh, and I shoot him one back that he's going to regret it if he does. Morris shrinks a bit in his chair.

Rudi raises his hand like he's back in class. Though in class he never would have raised his hand.

"Very good," Dad says, and we all go along with heads bowing and hands folding in anticipation of Rudi gracing us with his grace.

We have our heads down for probably thirty silent seconds.

I look up and find everybody else doing the same. Rudi looks around at everybody looking at him. He looks slightly more bewildered than usual. Then sheepish, shrugging and smiling.

"Rudi," I say, "do you want to do this?"

"Sure," he says. "Sure, sure."

We all bow our heads again.

We wait thirty silent seconds again.

Suddenly, Morris's voice fills the void.

"We thank you, Lord, for this wonderful meal and these wonderful people. And we ask that you see the four of us home safely from this great and serious adventure. Amen."

"Amen," say all of us.

"That was very nice," Mom says to Morris.

"Thank you," he says.

"What happened to you?" Beck asks Rudi.

He gets that same shy, embarrassed look and offers the palms-up gesture. "I didn't realize what that was. We never did that at my house."

"Why did you volunteer?" Dad wants to know.

"I didn't, sir. I was drafted."

Beck lowers his head again, prayerlike. Morris leans over and gives Rudi a supportive back pat. Mom looks at Dad. Dad looks to me.

"No, he's not joking," I say, shaking my head and grinning.

Dad looks, very concerned, in the direction of Rudi, who gives him a tentative smile in return. I hear my mother, under her breath, say, "Oh, God love him."

Dad folds his hands and leads grace, part two. "Lord, please do watch over and protect these brave young Americans through all their coming trials. Especially Rudi."

Which becomes our Amen.

"Especially Rudi," I say brightly.

"Especially Rudi," says Morris, says Mom, says Beck.

"Especially me," says Rudi, causing my father to burst out of character altogether, break ranks, and go over to give Rudi a mighty grab of both his shoulders and a squeeze firm enough to water the boy's eyes. Right there at the dinner table.

Nobody gets up here before dinner is finished without an ironclad, life-and-death excuse. Ever.

Oh, my.

The meal itself is a triumph, with my father loosening up considerably. Unlike most people, Dad gets more relaxed in the presence of a bunch of fighters than in a more peaceable crowd. And now he considers us fighters.

"You, Private Smarty-pants, come over here," he says to Beck once he has finished his main meal and his seconds.

Beck happily gets up, probably expecting some sort of award for cleaning his plate. He stands next to Dad, watching as the old man rolls up his crisply ironed sleeves.

"Wow," says Beck.

It's the tattoos. On his left forearm is the traditional seal of the United States Army, the one that's been around since the Revolution. It has two flags crossed, the thirteen-star American flag with another one that looks like it's got a floating empty suit and tie in the middle of it. There are various guns and cannons and spears and a small snake holding in its mouth a banner that says THIS WE'LL DEFEND. Really, the Army could have borrowed the seal from my dad rather than the other way around.

On his right forearm is a copy of a famous portrait of the Sioux chief Sitting Bull in white buckskins, looking hard and sharp straight at you, a single feather rising behind his head. A ribbon beneath the portrait reads WOUNDED KNEE.

Both Rudi and Morris are eager to join the viewing, and they get up from their seats. But Dad withers them both with a quick-shot look that practically radiates heat and drops them back in their chairs like a pair of ducks shot out of the sky.

"Oh," Morris says. "Permission to stand, sir?"

"Granted," Dad says. This is quite a party for him.

The boys rise again, only for Rudi to be shot back to earth again.

"Sorry," he says. "I thought that counted for both of us."

"Don't think, son," Dad says. He says it in a way that is totally different from how any of us would have said it. No joke, no teasing. He says it with warmth and sincerity and hope that Rudi will be able to take that really good advice with him into the Marines and carry it all the way right back to this table after it's all over.

"Yes, sir, I won't," Rudi says. "I mean, no, sir. Yes, sir." He looks at my dad with the scared puppy-in-love eyes that normally tell me that I am his hero.

"Oh, get over here, Rudi," Dad says, breaking protocol every which way now under Rudi's peculiar spell.

Just then my little brother, Caesar, comes bounding in and presents himself in the doorway.

"Oh, what part of the induction program are we at now?" he asks mischievously.

"Tattoo Worship," Mom responds with a giggle.

"Hah," Caesar says. "At least I haven't missed the

ritual buzz-cutting ceremony. I skipped dessert over at Nick's for that. And they were having Moon Pies."

"Ritual *what*?" Beck asks. Beck really likes his hair. It's auburn, halfway between curly and wavy, and hangs just below his ears. He is the closest we come in this group to anything approaching hippie.

"Regulation haircuts," Dad says, like he's Monty Hall pulling the curtain on *Let's Make a Deal*. "Professional *and* free."

I keep my hair pretty close to regulation as it is, so another sixteenth of an inch one way or another never matters much to me. Also, I knew this was coming. Now's the time for me to sit back and enjoy.

"Well," Morris says extra calmly, "don't they give us haircuts as soon as we report for duty?"

"Of course they do," Dad says. "But you want to make a good impression, right from the get-go. Like I did. The Army didn't even wind up giving me a haircut, after the one I gave myself."

Yes. Himself.

"Trust me, men. A good impression goes a long, long way when you enter the service, especially in wartime. The very last thing you want to do is show up looking like hippies, let me tell you."

Dad's hippie-ometer is set for ultrasensitive. He has considerably less patience for them than I have, and I have none at all.

"Who's first up?" Dad asks.

For the second time ever I see Rudi shoot his hand up into the air.

"Well done, my boy, that's the spirit," Dad says. He gets up and crisply leads a small procession out to the barbershop I know so well. That would be our back porch. Rudi is actually sort of marching, trying to stay in lockstep with my father, whose natural stride is a kind of march. Morris follows right behind, in a way that is completely descriptive of him. You can't quite tell if he is for or against what is happening, but there is a sureness to his commitment to it anyway. It's a sort of determined slouch in the direction of events.

Beck and I meet at the doorway at the same time, stopping to face each other. Caesar squeezes past us while Mom pats both our cheeks on her way to the kitchen.

"You'll love it," I say, grinning. "You'll feel like a new man. Hey, you'll feel like a man, period."

"No, I won't," he says.

"Oooh," I say, "is that a confession? I always had my doubts about you anyway."

He laughs. "After you," he says.

"No, after you," I reply.

Then we go through the door at the same time, calculating just right to get wedged in there, stuck together, arms flailing and making Mom dissolve in giggles.

A love for the Three Stooges is probably the strongest bond between Beck and me.

By the time we reach the porch, Rudi is sitting happily up in the big chair with a baby blue bath towel tucked around his neck. Dad is checking his hardware: sharp scissors, electric clippers, straight razor.

"So," Rudi chirps, sounding more like the barber than the client, "did you hurt your knee in the war, then?"

Morris is having trouble with patience. "Rudi, please, just get your hair cut without saying anything else."

"It's all right," Dad says, patting the top of Rudi's head. "I relish the opportunity to educate. Wounded Knee was the battle that represented the effective end of the Indian Wars. The end of that whole period of history when the native peoples still had a fighting chance to retain their land. And it was set off by the killing of Sitting Bull."

In silence then, my father starts cutting Rudi's hair.

"I wasn't even close then, was I?" Rudi says, and Dad just keeps on cutting.

The first cut takes no more than five or six minutes. I jump in next, and that takes maybe three. Caesar, not due for a trim for a solid week yet, jumps in and out just as quick. Then Morris gets his de-hippifying.

Dad gestures at the chair, dusting it off for the last appointment of the day.

"No, sir. But thank you, sir," Beck says. And if

respect were smoke we would all be choking now. Beck is not challenging my Dad here.

All the same I wish he would just get in the chair.

"You don't want a free haircut?" asks The Captain, formal as you please.

"Ah, get a free haircut for cryin' out loud," Morris says. *Just go along to get along* is what he'd like to say.

"Look, feel mine," Rudi says, pausing from feeling it himself just long enough to shove his dome in Beck's face. Beck rubs the dome, kisses it, then shoves it away again.

"You're just gonna lose it in a few days anyway," I say wearily. Beck is an exceptional guy who can be very hard to talk to sometimes.

"I know that," he says. Then he turns back toward the evening's host. "And I appreciate and respect your offer, sir. But I just feel like I need to fly my freak flag for just these few more days."

Ah . . . why? Why did he have to do that? He meant it as a joke, I know. He meant it to be playful, in a way that would get a fake-angry response, a challenge. Delivered in a way that said he was different from my father's world but not necessarily opposed to it.

In a way that my father could never, ever appreciate.

Caesar looks straight up in the air, then slinks into the house like he's doing the limbo under an invisible crossbar.

"Is that the flag you want to fly, young man?" Dad says, clearly working to maintain composure.

"Dad, Beck was just —"

He holds an index finger up in my direction. "Out of turn," is all he says.

"I am very sorry if I was out of line, sir," Beck says. He looks, for the moment, as he basically never looks — uncertain and nervous. "I did not in any way mean to offend you. You are a great man and a great host. I apologize for my lapse in manners."

The harmful electricity in the air starts buzzing just a little bit less now.

"Well, young man," Dad says, "you do deliver a quality apology, I'll give you that."

"Thank you," Beck says. "With my mouth, I've had to learn."

Dad bows, then gestures to the chair again.

Sheesh. No cease-fire yet.

"Sir, I just want to wear my hair a few more days. I want to wear it through the doors of induction and pledge my allegiance. I want to say my small piece for freedom of speech, which we Americans hold dear. Let's call this my First Amendment hair."

Holy smokes, do we have the two superpowers of blowhard going at it here?

Then suddenly Dad steps away from his barber chair. He walks, stern as Cochise, right up to Beck's face. Beck's face doesn't go anywhere, but I see the shakes on the inside of him threatening to come trickling out his eyes. I feel unable to move a muscle, and I am the toughest nonveteran here by some ways.

"Sir," Dad breathes into Beck's face. Never thought I'd feel like feeling sorry for Beck but, yup.

"Sssir?" Beck responds, clearly pronouncing those extra S's.

"First Amendment Hair certainly has a better ring than *freak flag*." Beck definitely catches a bit of the spittle of contempt on the end bit there.

We do a group exhale.

"Thank you, sir."

"And you have got a certain amount of courage. You will most definitely need it."

"Yes, sir," Beck says.

Dad extends his hand, Beck takes it. Dad holds him in his famous manly military death shake for several seconds.

Then the sound of the electric clippers, like a tiny little fighter plane, as Dad swings his left hand from behind his back, over his shoulder, swooping down on Beck.

Beck breaks away and stumbles toward the door and back into the kitchen.

I laugh, and Morris and Rudi join me as Dad proceeds to sweep up. It is mostly the laugh of relief, but it feels good.

"Go ahead in, boys," Dad says. "I'll clean up."

Morris holds the screen door open as Rudi goes in, then me. He puts a hand on my shoulder, pushing me in.

"Who says your dad doesn't have a sense of humor?" he says.

"Who says he was joking?" I say.

For the record, he wasn't.

Off the record, I'm ready. I've got my orders and I've got my baldy cut and I've got my head of steam. I want Boston in the rearview mirror and Vietnam in my sights. I want to get on with it.

I want to get these guys out of my house.

Rotten, right? I can't help it. This phase is over. This moment is over, and the moment I know that is when Rudi gets up off my couch, trailing oatmeal-raisin crumbs across my mother's nice carpet, and rubs Morris's head and makes a wish *for the sixth time tonight*. Everybody laughs. Again. Mom whips out her trusty carpet sweeper and cheerfully collects crumbs before they get ground in. Again. Dad addresses the troops, again, on one more of the many indigenous peoples of Southeast Asia and what we had better be on the lookout for. The guys hang on every word like they all add up to one greasy pole of dear life. Yes, for sure, The Captain has done his homework, but come on now.

"Do you see any parallels between any of these

tribes, sir, and the ones you know well among the American Indians?"

That question could come only from Beck.

And it could only bring me to one conclusion, as this is the only time in my knowledge that anyone has had to *prod* my father into more of this kind of thing.

They don't want to leave.

I should have seen it earlier, and I should be understanding about it now, and sure it makes some kind of sense, and yes these are my best pals in the world, but jeez, like I was saying, I am *ready*.

"Right," I say, standing up and clapping my hands twice, crisply. "I don't know what any of you are doing tomorrow, but I for one have an early and long day ahead. So . . ."

No rude boys here, I have to say. Crybabies and mama's boys, maybe, but the manners are grade A. Everyone is standing, milling, preparing to leave before the echo of my clap is even dead. Both Mom and Dad scramble out of the room with a sense of purpose.

We see that purpose when we tromp to the front hallway and find a small honor guard: Mom and Dad, on either side of the doorway, waiting to see the boys through. First through is Morris.

Dad shakes his hand so hard I can feel it five feet away. He winces just a bit.

"Bring the maximum of death to the minimum of people," Dad says. Morris then turns around to face my mother, who kisses him, hugs him, and hangs a scapular around his neck. It's like a fabric necklace with a sort of postage-stamp Jesus face hanging off it.

Beck steps up, and it feels a whole lot like Mass because my mother is all kinds of Catholic.

". . . maximum of death to the minimum of people."

It is a variation, anyway, on the Mass.

"Rudi," Dad says, his first diversion from the script. "Follow orders. Follow every single last order, son, and follow it all the way."

"Ow," Rudi says.

Mom kisses him, scapularizes him, hugs him for an extra-long time — about the time of the other guys combined.

My parents have done their thing and nod at me as they melt away. They are nodding that they know this is our moment. Me and my boys, finally . . . no, not *finally*, but for now having our farewell. Our time. When my parents go, I stand in the doorway, the three *other* stooges on my porch, under a yellow light and a squadron of moths.

We stare in silence. This is our *big moment*, apparently.

"See ya," I say.

Beck laughs out loud, waves me off, and starts down the stairs. Morris shakes his head in amazement, slaps me five, and follows. Rudi stands there, staring at me.

I stare back. "Follow orders," I say. "Go."

I snap off the light right over his head.

He stares.

They call for him to come, already pulling away.

I close the door on Rudi.

After a sleep slashed open with excitement, I am up with the crickets, still at it. I skip my parents' bedroom altogether just like I told them I would. I grab my bag and I head to my new life, my always life, my destiny.

I open the door to Rudi.

"Oh, man," I say.

No indication either way if he has been frozen in that spot all night or just managed to hit his spot precisely, but I don't care.

"I don't care," I say, sweeping right past him.

"I wanna talk," he says.

"Rude, y'know, I got something kind of important to do this morning."

He's at my heels like a puppy as I make my way down the street toward the bus station.

"I wanna talk," he says. "I can't believe you don't wanna talk."

"I don't wanna talk."

"I wanna talk."

"I don't wanna."

"I wanna."

Rudi loses at absolutely everything. Except this. He can do this forever.

"I don't wanna."

"You can't do that."

"I can do that."

"You can't."

I stop in my tracks, and he bangs right into the back of me. We converse just like this.

"There is nothing to talk about, Rudi. We're soldiers now. Fighters. We don't talk, we *do*."

He is pressed against the back of me, breathing on the spot where my brain stem meets my spinal cord.

"This is getting kind of weird, Rudi."

He continues doing what he's doing.

"Are you trying to communicate directly with my central nervous system? If you are, knock it off."

"I wanna go with you," he says, shaky. "I should just go with you."

I spin on him, somewhere between horrified and homicidal. I could choke him now, which may be the best thing for everybody.

I am even looking at his neck as I spin around, so I must mean it.

Then I see. He is wearing three scapulars.

"What's this all about?" I ask, reaching and fingering the Jesus Three.

"Beck and Morris decided these would make me a little more invincible," he says somberly.

"Well," I say, shrugging, "couldn't hurt, right?"

"Are you gonna give me yours now?" he asks.

"No, dodo, I'm not gonna give you mine. This was from my own *mother*, ya barbarian. How could I give that away? Anyhow, you got three Jesuses looking after you already. Just like you got the three of us looking after you already. Beck will be up in the sky, Morris will be floating off the coast, and I will be right there in the hills and jungles keeping an eye peeled for you every second. Anybody trying to shoot at you gets shot by me."

He pauses for thought. It's quick.

"I've been thinking about Canada a lot lately, Ivan."

My pause is even shorter. "Try and go to Canada and I'll shoot ya myself."

"At least that'll be quicker," he says.

I shake my head, knowing he would never run. I don't believe he would ever do that to his country. Or to Canada.

But even more, I know he wouldn't do it to me.

I check my watch. "I gotta go, man," I say, pulling him by his collar. "Come on and walk me to the station. I'll give you a big kiss good-bye for luck."

"Really?"

We walk, but I look back at him at the same time. His voice was alarmingly upbeat with that *Really?* so I try and read more of an explanation off his face. But his face is all over the place. He is delighted, scared, confused, lost, hopeful, and dejected.

We are right in front of the bus station.

"Oh, for the love of —" I say, and interrupt myself in order to stop, grab his pathetic, sad little face, and kiss him demented and hard on his cheek. "There ya go," I scold. "I will never do that again for as long as I live, so you better just cherish it. Be smart. Keep safe. Shoot the right guys, try not to shoot the wrong guys. Keep in touch. And come home to me with lots of great stories."

I shove him away from me, unable to carry my old friend anymore because jeez, I have got to do my own big thing now.

I spin on my way to the entrance and run right into this big biff of a local 4-F fatso frat boy who has been kicking around this town probably since my dad took this very bus trip. Toby.

"Move, Toby," I say.

"Can I have one?" Toby says, tapping his cheek and making kissy lips.

"If you mean one of these," I say, giving him a prime look at my big right hand.

He fakes a laugh and walks around me as I walk around him. Before I can enter the bus station I hear him again. "Can I have one?"

"No?" Rudi says, practically asking permission to not kiss the big stink of a guy. "Lemme go. Get off me. . . ."

I drop my bag, turn around.

"You know," I say, stomping back big-boy style, "I'm going to be late for the war."

Toby squares on me, making that infuriating little move, the *come on, bring it on* gesture with the waving fingers of both upturned hands. Sometimes I swear my own mother could coax me into a punch-up if she did that.

Good thing this ain't Mom.

I greet him with my full weight thrown behind a straight left hand. I have never landed a cleaner punch. My hips feel the aftershock. He straightens, and I punch him even harder with my right. Rudi is yelling something but I have no time for Rudi or words. I grab Toby with my left hand, hold his shirt tight while I shake him left-right-back-front 'til he is so off balance he doesn't know where he is going and can't land a punch.

But I know where he is going. And everywhere he goes he finds my knuckles. I punch him, mouth, mouth, eye, nose, mouth, until I drive him straight back, down, and over the top of Rudi himself.

I stand over the two of them, Toby holding his face together with his hands and Rudi half underneath him and smiling up at me like a dope.

"Dope," I say, offering Rudi a hand up. "You gotta learn to get out of the way. You *really* gotta learn to get out of the way."

He is still smiling.

I have to laugh a little, despite how much he's worrying me at the moment.

"What's up with you, numbskull?" I ask.

"Nothing. I just . . . feel a little safer all of a sudden. I feel good, Ivan."

"That's swell. I feel like we are right back where we started a million years ago, with me fighting battles for you."

"Yeah," he says, still beaming. "Cool."

I can't get away from him fast enough now.

"I gotta hurry," I say, scooping up my bag and opening the door to the bus station. "I gotta go kill everybody in Vietnam before you get there."

"Thanks," he calls, and I don't dare look back.

PART TWO

CHAPTER FIVE

Home on the Range

Not to be bragging or anything, but for about six and a half of the eight weeks of Army basic training, I could have run the whole show myself.

They opened us up with the same "challenge" we ended up with, the Physical Combat Proficiency Test. This starts with the hand-over-hand ladder test, where you have to carry yourself from rung to rung, doing thirty-six of them within sixty seconds. Then there is an obstacle course that is an insult to obstacles. Then there is the fun part, where you have to crawl on your belly through the dirt, from one end of the field to the other, in the allotted time. And last there is the mile run. They didn't tell me, but I am pretty sure I did the belly crawl faster than several guys did the run.

Anyway, while it might not have been backbreaking stuff, it was at least interesting and it was exercise and it got us all closer to the important stage: fighting the enemy. Well, not all of us. If you don't make enough points in the final round of tests, you don't graduate from boot camp with the rest of the platoon, and that means you get *recycled*. Right back to the beginning of camp to give the whole thing another shot.

There were five of those guys out of our platoon. I hope I never have to fight alongside any of them, ever.

The reward, after day five of week eight of doing everything the Army wants us to do, is we get to see our MOS posting — that's Military Occupational Specialty — to find out what the next stage of military life will bring our way. OJT, on-the-job training, is where we separate the desk jockeys from the grunts, the brainboxes from the cannon fodder. And not a minute too soon.

If the Army has decided to make it their business to please me, then they are off to a fine start. Putting me in the Marksman Program not only shows very good sense but has the added bonus of creating one mighty happy soldier.

And one ecstatic soldier's dad.

"Exactly!" The Captain says when I call him from the pay phone as soon as I read my posting. There are a lot of guys waiting to use this phone, but despite the staring and grumbling I still want to stretch this moment as much as I can. "Exactly, Ivan. See, the United States Army does indeed know just what it is doing despite what that know-it-all Walter Cronkite says. They spot talent, they don't mess around. They put that talent in position to flourish. You are going to go far in this career, boy, you just mark my words."

I am marking his words with a smile so big it hurts. Childish is what I am being, and so what.

My comrades don't completely agree with the *so what* part and begin actually rocking the phone booth.

"Dad, listen," I say, laughing probably more than I should with an angry mob watching me so closely, "I have to give up the phone to some of the other guys now."

"The *other* guys," he says, allowing himself to be a little bit less of the Army team player he normally likes to be. "How many of the *other* guys have been assigned to the Marksman Program? Answer me that."

"I can't answer you that, Dad, since I don't have the answer. I will try and find out for you for next time, though."

The rocking gets more furious now, and so does the pounding on the glass. I am feeling pressure on my back as I try to hold the bifold door closed. It is still good-natured enough, the harassment, but it feels like it could possibly be turning. And, marksmen or not, these are now trained soldiers I am ticking off.

"Okay," Dad says, though, really, hanging up now is not okay, and we both want it to go on forever. "I'll let you go, son. Go on, go on . . ."

"Thanks, Dad. Listen, I'll call —"

"I love you, Ivan," he blurts.

I stop smiling like a monkey. My heart pounds and, jeez, my eyes get all kinds of watered up. I just didn't see it coming at all, and now look at me, in front of all the men and everything.

It's just not done. Not like this. Not between us.

The whole Army seems to feel it, too, and the howling, pounding, rocking stops.

"I am very proud of you, son," he says, sniffing. Cripes. Sniffing.

"Yeah, Dad," is the absolute best I can do right now, but I know my best is good enough right now. "Yeah, Dad." Then, "Mom, huh?"

"I will," he says. "Of course."

It was eight hours a day on the rifle range during that last week and a half of basic that got me my assignment. I went straight from there, Fort Riley, Kansas, to my AIT — that's Advanced Individual Training — at Fort Benning in Georgia.

But while it was my shooting at Fort Riley that got me into the Marksman Program, it was my shooting from much earlier that got me where I am now.

"Where on earth did you learn to shoot like that, soldier?" asks my instructor, Sergeant Bing. I am lying on my stomach, shooting at targets on the five-hundred-yard range. "Boys from Boston don't show up shooting like that."

"New Hampshire, sergeant," I say, continuing my shooting. "With my dad. He was an Army captain in

World War Two. A hero. We have a small shack of a place way up in the woods there. I've been a shootist since I was five years old."

"Good hunting?"

"Mostly just small stuff. Squirrels, rabbits, coyotes. And hippies trying to run to Canada."

"Ha!" Sgt. Bing says. "Fire away, son. Fire away."

I do fire away, every day. I enjoy every minute of it and get better and better until it makes no sense to keep me any longer on American soil.

CHAPTER SIX

It's a Boat, Sir

After the long, long flight, we can smell it as we get nearer to the action in Vietnam.

I have been watching all the news and listening to all the stories and imagining my actual self there in the battle zone, but I have to admit this is not at all what I expected. The scent came into the plane during the last twenty minutes of our approach, but now as we come to a stop and the door opens and we take the stairs down to the airfield, it's even more of a shock. It smells — it tastes — like if you took all of high school during the last week of classes, put it into a blender, and boiled it on the stove. The sweat and hormones of gym mixed up with all the leftover grease and garbage of the Dumpsters outside the cafeteria, mixed with any and every chemical you could get together from the physical sciences lab — the ones they always told you were not to be combined under any circumstances. Plus the parking lot smell at the end of the day, with guys peeling out and leaving doughnuts of rubber, and three-quarters of the old rustboxes the seniors drive burning oil enough to give every student his own personal toxic cloud for keeps. All that blended together in the hottest, sweatiest heat under the sun combines to smack the face of every lucky soldier stepping off the plane.

I only get more excited.

We are led to a bus sitting baking on the asphalt by a noncommissioned officer who shouts and points and does not seem at all pleased to see us. The news keeps saying how badly the Army claims we are needed, but from the faces all around you would swear we were crashing a party we were not invited to.

It is a long ride in a bus with no air-conditioning and cage-lined windows. I have never traveled out of my time zone except for training in Kansas. This is so different in every way that I am sorely tempted to borrow from *The Wizard of Oz* and tell the guy next to me we ain't in Kansas anymore. But among the many fine tips my dad sent me off with was how easy a guy picks up a nickname in the service, and I do not want to spend the next four years as Dorothy.

But my, this ain't no Kansas. And for the first time I truly understand the meaning of jet lag.

So I look at that guy next to me, white-blond hair and six foot two of lanky. I see the same brain-dead, where-am-I-never-mind-don't-tell-me expression that I must be wearing. Without a word, I lean my head on the window and let it rest there.

"You know that wire is for Vietcong guerillas throwing grenades into buses like this one, don'tcha?" my lanky pal says. "They don't look no different from the regular civilians walking by."

I calmly pull my head away from the window and fall asleep with my chin on my chest.

I wake up when the bus *ker-thunks* to a stop and the troops start trooping, thumping their gear down the stairs into the bright sunshine.

"This ain't us," Lanky says as I shake my head and start out of the seat.

"Well, it ain't you," I say, a little put out by this, "but how do you know it ain't me?"

Lanky reaches out and fingers my dog tags in a strangely familiar gesture.

I slap his hand away instinctively.

"I read your name, man," he says, laughing. "They called out by name, and I thought since you were sleepin' so heavy I'd just leave you to it."

"Oh," I say. "Well, thanks."

"Pleasure to meet you, Ivan," he says, holding out a big bony hand.

"Pleasure to meet you . . ." I say, shaking with one hand and checking his tags with the other, which he apparently wants me to do. ". . . Laurence. I guess I'll be calling you Larry, then."

"Only if you want me smacking your butt all over Vietnam, Ivan," he says happily.

"Laurence," I say through a gritted smile.

Three-quarters of the population of the bus unloads at the base in front of us, a sprawling, flat, ugly, disposable-looking collection of buildings. The driver yanks the door shut, jams the old bus into gear, and tells us we have only a short way to go yet. As we pull away I watch the base fade behind us and think, *That is exactly what I expected the base to look like in every respect.*

Then, shortly as advertised, we pull up to our own new home.

And it is nothing at all what I expected it to look like.

"It's a boat," Laurence says flatly.

"It's a boat," I say flatly.

"Yo, driver, there must be some mistake," Laurence yells out as the man yanks the door open once more. "We are Army. Infantry. We don't live on no boats."

The driver laughs. "Well, you don't live on no bus, so get out. All of ya, come on, out ya go."

We all pile out and into the light and stand there staring.

"Welcome to the USS *Benewah*," says the sergeant, standing wide-legged in front of us with his hands clasped behind his back.

Instinctively, the twenty of us fall into a line, side by side by side, with our belongings at our feet.

"But it's a BOAT! SIR!" Laurence calls out, prompting muffled laughs up and down the line.

"Officer material," the sergeant says calmly.

Calmly? This surprises me a little bit. I expect a certain level of harshness, especially in the early going, from the noncommissioned officers. The NCOs are really the whips in the whole operation, making the vast numbers of lowly troops do the bidding of the Army — which you can trace all the way up the line right back to the brain of the commander in chief himself. And the usual way of keeping troops in line is with a constant barrage of verbal violence bordering on brutality. I expect it and almost feel a little let down here at not getting it.

Wrong-footed right off the bus. Can't be wrong-footed. Have to be ready for any-any-anything, even if it is an ambush of niceness.

"Yes, people, this is indeed a watercraft. The *Benewah* is your station. It is part of the Ninth Division's collaborative effort with the Brown Water Navy, a barracks ship that functions just the same as a regular land-based barracks, housing approximately thirteen hundred personnel, including officers if you choose to include them — which I, personally, do not."

Again there is a ripple of laughter, this time more open as guys get quickly more relaxed about it.

Except that I don't. Discipline is what the Army is about, what it stands for. What it stands *on*. I don't need the NCO to be my buddy, I need him to be my leader. And as for making jokes about the officers in front of these brand-new raw recruits . . .

"There a problem, private?" the sergeant screams in my face.

That's more like it.

"No, sir!" I shout.

"Well, then, why are you not laughing at things that I say that are obviously of a humorous nature?" he shouts.

"Because I am a trained soldier at attention, sir!"

The volume of the conversation drops when he sees I am taking this whole war thing kind of seriously.

"Fair enough, private," he says. "At ease, men." He starts walking up and down in front of us, then one by one shakes hands. "Now, you are going to encounter a great variance in the responses you get here in Vietnam, and I think it is an important part of my job to prepare you for some of that. Now, I, like all of you here, have been through CI school. That's why you are here. The soldiers stationed on the *Benewah* are largely involved in Counter Insurgency. You are going to have to figure out, on a daily basis, on an hourly basis, on a minute-to-minute basis, who are the friendlies, and who are the animals you have to blast right off the face of the earth on sight.

"But enough about the Marines . . ."

Now *there* is a joke I can laugh at. Wish Dad could have heard it.

"Seriously, though, this is a message you are not necessarily going to receive from a lot of other NCOs around here, so do listen up, take note, and do what you will with the knowledge."

Suddenly, even with the sweat beginning to run down along where my sideburns should be, I get a little chill.

"The men around you are among some of the finest you will ever want to meet, but to be frank, the experience of fighting here for an extended period has a big effect on even the toughest soldiers. There are fewer *lifers* in this Army than there are in the regular force, because of the need to staff the war and still rotate people out of here within twelve months' time. So you may find some people a little suspicious of you until they get to see what kind of soldier you really are. And, by the same token, you may feel the same way about the men you are required to fight alongside.

"There is going to be one primary thing about you, something that you are going to decide or that is going to be decided for you in the heat of action. And this quality is going to be figured out, in a hurry, by the men fighting shoulder to shoulder with you in the face of — let me tell you from personal experience — an astoundingly fearsome opposition. The question you have to answer is this: Do you want to kill for your country, for your fighting brothers? Do you want to *fight* your way through this or just *get* through it until your twelve months are up? You're going to be asked, in so many ways, are you a *shooter* or a *shaker*?"

I don't know if I will ever meet a simpler question my whole life. I am here to kill, and I know that. I am fine with that. I am all over that.

Sergeant stands there, looking us over, back in his troop-reviewing, semiofficial, wide-legged stance, hands clasped behind his back. He smiles broadly. Meanwhile, the bus that has brought us in is rapidly filling with soldiers it is bringing right back out again. There seems to be less tension in that population than in ours.

Suddenly, there is another, stiffer sergeant standing right behind him, carrying a full duffel bag. He starts nudging Smiling Sarge with the bag. Smiling Sarge does a quarter head-turn to look at Scowling Sarge, who scowls.

"What are you doing with my recruits?" asks Scowling Sarge.

"Toughening them up," says Smiling Sarge.

"Last call!" shouts the bus driver. "Destination: Oakland, California!"

The bus erupts with cheering. Smiling Sarge turns and grabs the bag from Scowling Sarge, who gives him a strong and — if it is possible — warm salute. Smiling Sarge simultaneously grabs him in a painful-looking crush of a hug around the neck.

"This is not Standard Operating Procedure, sergeant," says the sergeant, slightly strangulated.

"That's because *I* am no SOP, sergeant," says the smiler, before breaking away with a big wave and a "good luck" to all of us.

I believe we solved the mystery of the uncommonly happy noncom.

Which is not what we face now. Oh, no we don't. No mystery, and no uncommon happiness.

"STOP! SMILING!" are the first two words we get from our new leader.

It feels like an order that is supposed to last exactly twelve months.

CHAPTER SEVEN

Remain the Landscape

MORRIS,

I CANNOT BELIEVE IT. ALL THIS TIME, MY WHOLE LIFE, REALLY, I WAIT TO FINALLY ARRIVE AT WAR WITH THE ARMY...AND IT TURNS OUT TO BE THE NAVY! NO JOKE, MAN, I AM STATIONED ON THIS BIG MOTHER OF A BARRACKS SHIP CALLED THE BENEWAH THAT IS PART OF YOUR NAVY'S RIVERINE ASSAULT FORCE. THEY DID PAINT THE SHIP OLIVE GREEN, WHICH IS A NICE TOUCH AND REMINDS US THAT THE NINTH DIVISION IS STILL ARMY, JUST HERE TO BAIL YOU BOYS OUT WITH STUFF YOU CAN'T HANDLE.

AND ANOTHER THING. TURNS OUT THIS TUB IS A CONVERTED LST — THAT IS LANDING SHIP, TANK, JUST IN CASE THEY HAVEN'T TAUGHT YOU THAT IN THE NAVY — FROM WORLD WAR II. I MEAN, IT JUST MIGHT BE THAT I AM LYING HERE INSIDE A SHIP THAT BROUGHT MY DAD AND HIS MEN OVER TO SAVE THE WORLD TWENTY-WHATEVER YEARS AGO. AND EVEN BETTER, THE THING WAS BUILT AT THE NAVAL SHIPYARD RIGHT IN BOSTON.

IT ALL FEELS SO RIGHT, DOESN'T IT, MORRIS? LIKE
WE ARE SUPPOSED TO BE RIGHT HERE, RIGHT NOW?
HEY. WHAT ABOUT RUDI? SHOULD I FEEL GUILTY

I tuck the letter under my pillow. I will finish it later. Or not, maybe. Sometimes you feel like you have done a letter just by writing it, maybe, and sending it's not so important. Sending it is kind of weak, even.

And anyway it's not time for yakking, it's time for work.

We are stationed at a port called Vung Tau, which is on a peninsula in the South China Sea. It is the point at which all the fun of this war just begins to open up. But there is an undeniable crossroads feel to the place that tells me this is a transitional area, a Navy area, and that we, the Ninth Infantry, are intended for bigger and better things farther in-country.

So the initial days and duties have the feel of one last bit of on-the-job training before we get into the deep heat somewhere else.

I am assigned to a patrol. We have two express objectives, which are commonly referred to as H&I. That stands for Harassment and Interdiction. One of the greatest problems the American forces have been encountering, especially in these two most southern zones, 3 and 4, has been the consistent, successful, relentless supplying of insurgent cells down deep within the territory of South Vietnam. These fighters exist unseen within the dense jungles and riverbanks of the region and seem to be equipped with an endless supply of munitions to assault our forces with. We know the general supply lines that exist from the North on down, but the system is so sophisticated and cunning that the only effective way for us to deal with it is a constant infusion of men and weapons of our own right into the very arteries of the country: the big river ways and the small ones. The foliage, the hills and mountains and swamps.

So my home, my office, Region 4, is where we patrol, at the bottom end of South Vietnam. It contains sixteen different provinces, the whole of the mean Mekong Delta, and over fifty percent of the country's entire population. In the midst of all this life, we sneak in, look for secret supply deposits, and sit in ambush for the guys responsible for this whole big, bloody mess.

If a guy can't get motivated for that last part, then he's got no blood running through him.

"I do hope you are ready for everything and anything," Lieutenant Systrom says as our boat is lowered into the river. There are twenty-five of these fiberglass assault boats attached to the *Benewah* for the use of the Army exclusively.

"If we get anything less than everything and anything, lieutenant, I will be very disappointed," I say, to his apparent pleasure.

He shakes his head and smiles. "I see. I've got one of *them* on my hands," he says.

"You do, indeed," I say. "Whatever *them* are, I am one of them."

"That's great. I always say, if I had more fighters like that . . . I'd have less fighters like that. You boys are all great. Until you get yourselves shot to pieces."

"I won't be getting shot, sir."

"How do you know that?"

"I just know," I say.

Shakes his head again. Smiles again.

"Listen. I love the gung ho, I really do. But I need to know now if you're a listener. A lot of guys here, they're ready to fight but not ready to listen. Really, it works best if you're both ready to fight and ready to listen, because I could have some things to tell you that will help you to fight longer."

"I am a military man, lieutenant. As is my father, as was his father. I was bred to listen."

"That is what I wanted to hear," he says, and as our boat motors away, he leads me over to the rest of our small team. We sit and get better acquainted as we ease along the brown Mekong River.

Our gang of six includes the lieutenant; two corporals, Parrish and Lightfoot; and two more privates like me, Arguello and Kuns.

"Welcome aboard the *Ship o' Fools*," Lt. Systrom says,

and the guys all laugh. "By the way, that title is ironic. My guys are famously smart, cool under pressure, brave but not stupid. Does that describe you, Private Bucyk?"

"It does," I answer.

"Does that describe you, Private Kuns?"

"It does," says Kuns.

"Good, glad to hear it. Now that we have established that the two new guys are not idiots, let's get down to it."

Lt. Systrom shoves an M-79 grenade launcher in my direction. I did receive some instruction with the M-79 but not a great deal. I am in fact a little surprised it's still in use, as I had heard it was phasing out. At any rate, this is not the weapon of a sharpshooter.

"Oh, lieutenant," I say helpfully, "I should tell you, I am a graduate of the Army Marksman Unit."

The *Ship o' Fools* erupts with laughter, and it is clear who the fool is.

"And I should tell you, Private Bucyk, that every butt in this boat is a graduate of that same fine institution. I don't work with anything but. Now, every soldier in my group does time with every weapon in our box. I like versatility. Any problem with that?"

"No, sir, lieutenant."

"Glad to hear it," he says.

"*Ship o' Sharpshooters* is more like it," Arguello says. "Maybe we get a prize at the end for wasting the fewest bullets and the mostest VC."

The jolliest tub in the Army laughs a little more. Me, I can't help hearing my dad's words saying almost the same thing with no humor at all: *Bring the maximum of death to the minimum of people.*

I take the heavy, stumpy weapon and hand over my standard Army-issue M-16. The 40-mm grenade launcher is in its own way a pretty impressive thing, and it is immediately clear why it's known as The Thumper. It looks and feels like a single-barrel, large-bore, sawed-off shotgun. With this, and my pistol and my knife, I may not be a sharpshooter, but I don't feel defenseless, either.

My eyes go wide as Lt. Systrom makes another trade. The other new guy, Kuns, hands over his M-16 and in return gets the beast that has mostly replaced the launcher I am holding. The M-203 is a leaner, meaner version of the M-79 grenade launcher *combined* with the M-16A1 automatic rifle. When I was a kid lying in bed, thinking about wars and seeing myself in them — which I did a lot — this is the very type of beautiful piece of kit I saw myself marching into battle with. An involuntary small, hungry grunt comes out of me as it passes by.

"You'll get your shot," Lt. Systrom says.

Corporal Lightfoot gets an M-60 machine gun, while the other guys remain with their faithful M-16s.

But the boss has something special.

The lieutenant looks off in the distance, toward where we are headed, as he absently stands his gun up in front of him.

I know this gun. I have studied this gun. I have had many impure thoughts about this gun.

It is the M-21 Sniper Weapon System, and it is as beautiful as an Army weapon gets. It is long and sleek, with a high polish and a starlight scope perched on top for day and night hunting.

It's a hunting rifle. 'Cause that's just what it's for.

"Are you ogling my M-21?" Lt. Systrom says with a sly side glance.

I pull back, like I've been caught at something forbidden. I do tell the truth, though.

"Absolutely, sir."

Again I provoke laughter, but it is a more familiar thing now. This population agrees with me completely on this.

"Get in line, boy," Corporal Parrish says to me. "There ain't a man here who wouldn't shoot everybody else for a day with that beauty."

"Guess I should be worried, huh?" says the lieutenant.

"Sir," I say tentatively, "could I just handle the weapon for a minute?"

"Private Bucyk, you most certainly may —"

Pop! Pop-pop-popopopopopopopopop!

The early morning air is cut up with rifle shots coming at us from maybe two hundred yards inland. Every man hits the deck. Cpl. Lightfoot fairly lights up the entire jungle with machine-gun fire. The other guys pepper the area blindly with rifle shots. It is a bright and sunny morning and there isn't much hope of seeing where the shots are coming from. Muzzle flashes are faint, and these guys are good with the foliage, because there doesn't seem to be any movement out there anywhere.

"Private Bucyk!" Parrish screams at me. "Do you know what you are supposed to be doing with that thing, or does somebody need to help you?"

"Oh," I say like a simpleton. "Oh, yes, sir." I had made the cardinal error, already, of letting myself get overwhelmed and watching the action. My father would slap me stupid right now.

"Private Kuns!" Parrish yells, louder. "Grenades! We have enough shooters. Grenades!"

And, as if it has all been perfectly coordinated for Kuns and me to be arriving in-country and making our mark on it at the same exact time, we both let off our big mother grenades simultaneously, listen to them whistle across the sky, and watch them land in the same spot.

Bu-boo-oom!

There is an instant decrease in incoming fire, but not enough to feel safe. A round tears right through the side of the fiberglass boat, goes right between me and Kuns, and exits the other side. I can feel the rush as it passes.

I can feel that rush, and every other rush. I am pumping enough adrenaline to power the whole *Benewah* all by myself.

"More! Again!" Parrish screams, and I begin to wonder if he is actually the man in charge here. Then I look over to where Lt. Systrom is knuckled down, set up like a sniper as best he can over the lip of the boat. He is coiled, frozen, not firing — not breathing as far as I can tell.

The Navy boy piloting the boat begins a wide sweep away from the shore, which tears the lieutenant right out of his trance.

"What are you doing?" he shouts.

"Avoiding fire, what does it look like?"

"No, no, no!" Systrom screams. He points to the shore. "Your job is to get us in there so that we can do *our* jobs. We are Army, mister, not Navy, so you just get us onto land to do our jobs — then you can run wherever you like."

The Nav begins a swing back, and Lt. Systrom keeps pointing.

"*Into* the fire?" our pilot calls dubiously.

"*Straight* into it," our commander commands.

We go in, as all-guns-a-blazin' as it is possible to get, straight into the enemy fire, which is now clearly coming at us from two nests up the hillside. I aim a grenade at one nest. Kuns follows up, and the explosions sound to me like the "1812 Overture" the Boston Pops plays outside on the Charles River every July Fourth. We are all crouching, squatting, ducking as we try to fight the invisible when, finally, Systrom joins in.

Craaack.

His gun sounds nothing like anybody else's. It is subtle, crisp, sure. It is the gunshot equivalent of an Olympic diver hitting the water without a ripple.

The return fire is now reduced to almost nothing.

Looks like our head shot off their head.

We hit the bank going a little bit too hard, and everybody tumbles around for a few seconds. Then we compose, focus, and hop out of the boat one at a time and all out.

The Navy guy scoots off quick and says he will come back when we radio him and not before.

Lt. Systrom squats down under a short palm tree. He coolly goes over his map with Cpls. Parrish and Lightfoot while the rest of us continue to pound the remaining nest that only now is lights-out.

"Here is what we know," Systrom says. "Last night's recon indicates action here and here and here along this trail. That means you're probably gonna find drums."

The "drums" are the fifty-five-gallon metal oil drums that the enemy fills with arms and ammunition for the insurgents, then seals and buries in the bush. They are a big problem for us.

Systrom continues. "I'll take Kuns with me and find a perch right around here, high enough to oversee your whole area. Stay within these parameters and try to cover the whole length of the trail by dusk. Right?"

"Right," I say, all chirpy even though nobody asked me directly. I have never been as buzzy as I feel right now. This trail ahead of us is the very definition of the scary unknown. It is a mad, insane, helter-skelter thrill, and I feel at this moment like I want to run up that trail and personally flush out every sneaky Vietcong murderer, pull him out of his hole like a rabbit. I feel like these guys are holding me back.

At this moment it occurs to me that it is *easy* to be brave.

"Are you listening?" Cpl. Lightfoot says, nose to nose with me right now.

"Sorry, corporal," I say.

"You just calm those red eyes of yours right down now, *brave*. Understand me? It would be a shame to waste all of this on your first and last day out, right?"

"Right, corporal."

What I had, in fact, missed there was that we were going up the trail in twos, and I was to be paired with Lightfoot, while Parrish and Arguello would head up about ninety seconds in front of us.

We stand there, guns raised, eyes left-right-left, like marching, as the first two begin the slow, sweeping walk up the trail.

"Okay," Lightfoot says, "on we go."

The trail itself looks like it is built for a couple of bikes riding side by side, or maybe a little Japanese car. As Lightfoot and I walk, we can't quite reach out our hands and touch, but we can do it with our guns. We won't try it, though.

But it is close enough for whispering.

"So, what are you?" he says to me. I stare at him, wondering if he just has nothing real to say or if he is slowly rolling out the longest conversational time filler he can think of.

"I'm an American," I say.

"Great," he says, "but I mean more specifically. Like, you're a Catholic, obviously, from the doohickey around your neck. . . ."

"Scapular," I whisper-snap. "It's called a scapular, and I got it from my mother as I was headed off to here."

"That's nice. Most of The People, though, they don't go with the Catholic thing."

"What *people*?"

Up ahead, Parrish whirls around like a big, angry, armed ballet dancer. He mimes *shush*, then points at me with a bit of aggression.

"The People, man," Lightfoot says with a knowing smile. "What's your tribe?"

Now I really go goggle-eyed at him. I even crane my neck in his direction. He mimes *eyes front* by pointing two fingers at his own eyes, then pointing them up the road.

"Wow," I say. "I mean, that's pretty impressive. I don't even know how much Indian blood I've —"

"One quarter."

I open my mouth wide to give him a double *wow*, but he cuts me off.

"I was just kidding that time. But I see you got something in you somewhere. Tribe?"

I sigh, thinking about my dad's scattershot enthusiasm for the whole deal.

"My dad says Sioux, but —"

"Pfshht" is the noise that comes out of Lightfoot. It is not a noise of agreement.

"You are East Coast. I would guess Iroquois, but I could be wrong. Not as wrong as your father, of course . . . no offense."

"No offense. Somewhere right now my mom is laughing over this."

Both Parrish and Arguello stop suddenly and turn toward us, their guns raised. They stand facing into bushes as we catch up.

When we get there, we can see what has caught their

attention. About twelve feet off to the left of the small path, at the end of an even smaller path, is a mound. It is only slightly raised, but it seems different from the surrounding ground and a bit too carefully arranged. Lightfoot and I stand guard as the two of them advance. I draw my pistol and watch the road behind us while Lightfoot watches ahead.

There is about five minutes of digging before they indicate they have something. They dig faster now, a little less cautiously, until they get to the big metal drum and open it . . .

. . . to find it empty. Parrish curses, and we come in to have a look.

The side of the drum has been pried open and emptied, the remaining shell lying there opened like it is laughing at us. We waste about another two minutes staring before we trudge back out to the trail to start all over again.

The day goes mostly like that — a slow, methodical creeping through a hostile jungle where we do not encounter one other human being. As the hours pass and we edge farther out into the nothing, a strange combination of boredom and increasing fear creeps up into me. This, I find, I do not like.

We are at the perimeter of the area we are supposed to cover, having uncovered one other empty barrel and one empty hole where a barrel surely once was. I am weary in a way none of the basic-training stunts ever got me weary. This jungle is the hottest thing I have ever encountered, and it is heavy with a humidity that would keep me glistening with sweat even if I had a tap on my side for running it off of me. We're sitting, taking small sips of water, resting a bit for the return, when Lightfoot sees a configuration of fallen tree trunks that doesn't agree with him.

"Cover my back," he says, and I follow him to the trees about twenty feet away.

Once there, he starts making *hmmm* noises and clicks with his tongue a sound that says he is on to something that he does not want to be on to. The other two catch up, and Arguello starts immediately helping pull the trees apart. I make a move to go in with them, and Parrish grabs my arm. I look, and he just shakes his head no. Parrish and I watch each direction of the road and I, for some reason, have both my grenade launcher and my pistol trained on the trail.

"Oh, no," Lightfoot says. "No, no."

"Jeez," Arguello says.

"Again," Parrish says, disgusted. "How are they doing this? They are beating us to it every time, man, and I don't know how —"

He shuts himself right up as he reaches the site. I hear him breathing deeply, four, five, six times, and then I step up next to him.

And for a few moments I don't hear anything at all. It is, literally, like my hearing has been punctured dead.

Dead. There are three — and you can just about make it out because of the partial views of three heads — three dead men in this fifty-five-gallon drum.

Arguello puts his hand over his mouth, stands there as long as he can through one or two partial retches until vomit is bleeding out between his fingers, and heads for a tree to be properly sick.

"Keep it *quiet*," Parrish snarls as Arguello moans, low and chunky.

They are local people, or at any rate not US military personnel. They are dressed, as I have seen countless indigenous Vietnamese, in simple cotton togs. They are — were — small men, but not small enough to fit in there together. Not unless someone broke them badly.

Lightfoot is kneeling, like a priest, aside the drum. He touches, briefly and lightly, two fingers on each bloody skull. Then he looks up at me and Parrish.

"I'm guessing we just met our informants for all these munitions dumps."

He looks back and stares at them good long minutes more. Arguello is back with us but mostly looking away. Parrish is silent now, silent beyond being quiet.

"What do we do?" I ask finally.

Lightfoot looks up to Parrish, who has one hand covering the whole lower half of his face.

"Radio Lieutenant?" Arguello says into the void.

Parrish just shakes his head.

"You know Systrom," Lightfoot says. "If you radio him when he's locked in, it better be a life-or-death scenario."

"Or it'll *be* a life-or-death scenario," Parrish says through his hand.

"So?" I ask.

"I think we gotta leave 'em," Parrish says.

Lightfoot shakes his head.

"It's hard enough not being detected out here without also dragging a barrel full of —"

"Hey," Lightfoot interrupts.

Parrish just nods and holds a hand up. "But . . . I don't know, man."

"We don't take no barrel. We remove these men, individually, as individuals. And we carry them. We've already seen this whole trail. There should be no great trick to getting back okay."

Parrish ponders.

"Your call, corporal?" Parrish asks.

"My call, corporal."

All agreed, Lightfoot turns back to the men in the drum. "Sorry," he says down low as he begins delicately unpicking limbs from limbs, feet from mouths, noses from eyes.

————————— ★ —————————

"Corporal Lightfoot," I say as we near the end, the meeting point with the lieutenant.

"Yes, Private Bucyk?"

We are talking as softly as the puffing, dead Vietnamese summer air now. We are doing it without even trying because we couldn't possibly do anything more strenuous.

"My guy is starting to smell really bad."

"I am sure he feels the same about you."

Dusk is coming down quickly, and we can just barely see Lt. Systrom and Pvt. Kuns at the side of the trail in the distance. By my count I have shifted this man, this poor, worthy fighter, from one shoulder to the other thirty times. With the four of us ambulatory and the three of them along for the ride, we have each had periodic breaks, yet this has turned out to be backbreaking stuff. Especially with the requirement to stay on watch all the way down the road in case we missed anything the first time or anything new has popped up. Just keeping weapons at the ready is grueling in itself.

I can see the lieutenant's scowl from fifty yards. It adds to the weight of the casualty to the point that I just about fall down at the boss's feet when we meet.

"What's this?" Lt. Systrom asks, and his look doesn't suggest any answer is the right answer. "You had a duty. And picking up locals, however unfortunate those locals might be, was not part of that duty. So I ask again, why did I send out four men and get seven in return?"

Lightfoot does not waste words in his answer, reducing it, in fact, to just the very basics.

"Montagnards, sir."

The way he is leaning up on his toes and forward, Systrom looks like he has a strong response prepared. Then he retracts.

He stares at Lightfoot, nods, and pulls up the radio.

We continue the heavy march, back toward our landing spot as the lieutenant calls for our ride.

As we lift the last body, then the last of ourselves into the same bullet-holed fiberglass boat that got us here, I feel practically boneless myself. I stumble into a seat next to Lightfoot as the boat motors out onto the river. I look around at everybody looking the same as me. Though not as much as me.

I am a rookie and feel it.

"Lightfoot?" I say into the corporal's ear. "What's Montagnards?"

"Our friends," he says.

"Okay . . . right. Lightfoot . . . ?"

"Shhhh," he says, and pushes my face away. But gently.

———————— ★ ————————

Now I know.

I thought I knew fear, but now I know it.

I thought I knew horror, but now I know it.

I thought I knew tired . . . holy smokes, I thought I knew tired. . . .

"Private Bucyk," Lt. Systrom says from behind me as I'm just about into the mess for some dinner.

"Yes, sir?" I say, turning and saluting.

"I just wanted to check in and see how you thought operations went today. Your first real action. It's not like they tell you it's going to be, is it?"

"Not even close, sir. If they told me it was going to be like today on my first day, well, I just would have thought they were pulling my leg."

"Right, well, now you know. Truth is, pretty much every one of your days is going to be a lot like today."

I gulp. I know he can hear me gulp. That can't stop me from gulping again.

"Sorry, kid, I should have been more specific. I meant *my* day today. I lay motionless as a hibernating turtle, covered in leaves on the top of a hill, all day long. Never saw anything to shoot at. Hardly even blinked. That starlight scope, by the way, gets awfully tiresome on the ol' peep eye after a while."

"I . . . would imagine it does, sir."

I would also imagine he is telling me this stuff for a

reason, but I cannot for the life of me figure out what that reason might be.

"I bet you're hungry," he says.

"I absolutely am, lieutenant."

"And here I am, keeping you from your hard-earned meal after a long first day in the field. What's wrong with me? Tell you what — go on in there and eat, get your fill, then meet me back out here afterward so we can have a talk. How's that?"

"That is fine, Lieutenant Systrom. Sure."

"Great, then. See you right here. What say, half hour, yes?"

"Well, sir, I was thinking more —"

"Half hour, tremendous. See you here."

Now I'm worried all over again. Am I in trouble? Am I not in trouble? Does he like me? Is he taking me under his wing? Is he taking me outside to see what kind of man I really am?

Jeez, what am I worried about? What's happened to me? I never used to worry about anything. That's what was great about me.

Now I'm worried about being worried.

I look all around me before I step through the door of the mess. Nobody is watching, thank goodness.

I give myself such a belt across the face, I am sure my dad hears it and is smiling in my direction.

"There," I say. "That's better."

Thirty minutes of wolfing later, I encounter the lieutenant standing right where he said he'd be. He has his beautiful sniper's M-21 at his side.

"Fine, fine," he says, looking at his watch as I walk up to him.

"If you don't mind, sir, could I use the latrine before we begin?"

"Absolutely, private. I mind very much. Next time, plan your allocation of those thirty minutes more judiciously. Follow me."

Okay, then. I follow right behind as Lt. Systrom marches double-time through the compound, past the commissary and the NCOs' club and the BOQ, which is the Bachelor Officers' Quarters. Right past the dock and the boats all parked next to the big *Benewah*, out to the clearing where we have a makeshift six-station, three-hundred-yard firing range.

Lt. Systrom hands over the magnificent weapon, and my heart goes all beehive on me. I lift it, get a feel for it, raise the scope to my eye, and see that target through the early evening dark as clear as if it were about to bump into me. Already I feel like the rifle and I are one unit.

"You do know your way around a gun, don't you, Bucyk?"

"I believe I do, sir."

"You have dreams of being a sniper, don't you, Bucyk?"

"I have those dreams every night, sir."

"It is about so much more than shooting, you know, private. So, so much more. It is about stealth. It is about being a leaf in the forest rather than a baboon. It is about staying so quiet and so still for so long at a time you forget your own presence."

"Yes, sir, I know this, sir," I say, training the scope from one target to the next to the next and feeling I am the gun.

"So why did I spend all day today listening to you?"

I am no longer the gun.

"Sir?" I say, lowering the weapon to consider him.

"Your voice, Private Bucyk. All day long. From my high perch, my position of stealth, I listened to the sound of your voice from the farthest reaches of the trail."

"I was whispering, sir."

He is unimpressed with my defense, if he has even registered it.

"You see, being seen and heard in this line of work in this part of the world in this moment in history is the same as being dead. I have received very strong advance reports on you, private. I would like to not see you dead."

"I would like to not see that, either, sir."

"Well, if there were any serious enemy activity along that trail today, Bucyk, you would, in fact, be dead. Raise that weapon again and focus on the target."

I do, and I do, and I am loving it again.

"The possibilities are great for you, soldier. The possibility that you never get there is far greater. But for right now, I want you to focus on that target. Stay focused on that target. Do not make a sound. Do not twitch a fiber. Do not have so much as a detectable brain wave until I return to tell you otherwise. Is that perfectly clear?"

I have my flaws, but I am certainly not untrainable. I learn.

I do not respond in any way.

"Good," he says, and marches away again.

It seemed simple enough.

Stand, aim, point the gun at the target. I can't think of any more natural thing to do.

But thirty minutes in, I feel it. The pain starts at the top of my right shoulder. Then it grows, travels, radiates down my arm and up into my neck. There is a nerve toward the back of my neck that feels like someone has gotten in there with a pair of needle-nose pliers, has pinched it off, and is twisting, twisting, twisting like the elastic in those old balsa-wood propeller planes I used to build all the time.

My eye, the one I have on the target, has the sensation of a tiny hand scratching, the fingernails clawing lightly at the surface of the eye, then salty breath puffing lightly into it. I am sweating like I am personally the very source of the Mekong.

And I regret that missed latrine break more than any decision I ever made.

It has to be three hours before I hear footsteps coming my way. As they get closer it appears there are at least three, maybe four people coming. Relief, I am sensing relief, feeling relief, whether they are here to literally relieve me or not.

"Look at this disciplined piece of Army machinery here," Parrish says, walking around me like he's checking out a new car. Please don't kick my tires.

"Very impressive," Lightfoot says. "Do you suppose he's trying out for the LRRPs?"

The LRRPs are Long Range Reconnaissance Patrollers, and they are legendary as the most maniacal people in the entire show. They go out all painted up for night patrols as far out into the scarylands as they can get, remaining frozen for hours at a time to capture or terrorize individuals and bring back useful information or guns or enemy combatants as a kind of bonus.

"Nah," Arguello says. "One of his eyes is closed. LRRPs never close their eyes."

I don't care. Whatever they want to do to me now, I don't care because I am right now doing the most important job in the Army, the war, the world. I can see the three of them, walking around me, trying to get me to move, react, *exist* in a physical way that I am just not going to do even if it kills me.

Maybe I will lose my mind and wind up a LRRP at the end of it all.

No, I won't. Because I am not a LRRP. I am a marksman, and I am going to be a sniper.

"Would you like a drink?" Parrish asks, taking a long and theatrically slurpy sip off of what I think is ginger ale.

Moxie. All I can think of right now is Moxie. I miss Moxie. I want Moxie. When I get through this, I am going to make it my mission to secure a supply of Moxie. Moxie is my secret, my strength, my source. Moxie is my essence, and with it I cannot fail.

Lightfoot actually comes up close and blows on the side of my face softly. I have no idea what kind of torture this is intended to be, but it feels like heaven.

Arguello comes around the front of me and starts making sniffing noises.

"I don't remember this guy smelling like that when he got here," he says. "Smells like he's rotting. Do you think he is rotting since he got here?"

"Yeah, now that you mention it," Parrish says, "there is a little something foul going on there."

"Is it coming from here?" Arguello says, crouching down right in front of me.

My arms are screaming with the pain now. My neck is going to snap. I can't feel my hands.

After examining the area for several seconds, Arguello pulls a rolled-up magazine out of his back pocket. He begins to *fan* my already damp crotch area.

Oh, no. Oh, please, no.

I can feel the breeze coming through my clothes. I can feel the cool, can feel the humidity turning to frost as he fans faster and faster.

"Oh, man," Arguello says, jumping away like I was one of the deadly bamboo vipers that are everywhere here.

"Jeez," Parrish says from just behind me, "it's worse on this side."

They howl, they flail around, laughing and gagging and carrying on like evil circus clowns. I hear them getting farther away behind me, and I don't think I have ever been happier at the prospect of aloneness.

"You're doing great, kid," Lightfoot says in my ear before he, too, melts away.

I stand there, in my reek, but frozen in position as I hear the last of their sounds trail off. I don't know if I could relax my position now if I wanted to. A live version of rigor mortis seems to have gripped me at this point.

It is dead silent. I wait for more footsteps to come and none come.

"Very impressive" comes the voice from about three feet behind me, and the shock is nearly enough to make me twitch. But I don't.

"If I didn't know better, private, I would swear you were a part of the landscape. Except for the smell, of course. Since there are no skunks in this neck of the woods, I do believe you would have given your position away to any hostile troops within one kilometer."

Lt. Systrom walks around to the front of me.

"And this is just the beginning, Bucyk. With skill like yours, shooting people is the easy part."

It would be pretty easy at this moment, is what I'm thinking.

"But not only do you not have all the necessary traits of the true sniper, you don't even look the part. You look more like Daniel Boone trying to pick off Injuns than a modern-day precision killing machine. Now, I want you to get down on the ground, take up a proper sniping position, and get a bead on that hostile target there for real."

The Tin Man in *The Wizard of Oz* had less trouble moving after rusting in the forest all those years than I have right now. But I do it. I lower the rifle, feel the muscles in my shoulders, back, arms, hamstrings, moving more like steel cables and pulleys than real organic human parts. My pants feel all the more disgusting for the movement.

But I get down, stretch out, fold down the two bipod legs at the front of the M-21, and set my starlight scope on my enemy.

"Good," Systrom says. "Bet that's a relief, huh?"

I say nothing.

"Good," he says, then wanders off to the tree line alongside the range. I hear him rustling around in the trees for a minute but can't figure what he's up to until he comes up and drops a full load of camouflage foliage on top of me. He spends a few seconds spreading big palm leaves and sticks and branches over me in what must be a lovely naturalistic arrangement.

"Remain the landscape, soldier. Keep at it until you don't exist any longer. Or until I come back and tell you, whichever comes last."

I listen to his crisp, marching steps, and it seems like he takes forty-five minutes and several thousand strides before he clears the area. It does in fact feel like something of a relief to be off my feet and to have my arms supported. My elbows are stuck into the moist and loamy-smelling turf, which is a whole lot better than the air that was holding me up before.

But after an hour I forget how much better I feel.

After two hours I feel nothing in my hands, my arms, my legs. My neck is hurting again.

After three hours, I feel nothing, anywhere, inside my body as well as out. Only my eye feels like an actual physical part of this world.

"I almost tripped right over you," Lt. Systrom says, walking between me and the target.

Click.

I pull the trigger.

"Correct response," he says, clapping his hands together one loud time as the birds in the distant trees sing up the beginnings of the tropical-dawn chorus.

"You were so good I almost forgot where I planted you. Truth is, I did forget about you. Meant to be here an hour ago. Sorry, soldier."

It was very smart to leave the gun unloaded.

"On your feet, Private Bucyk."

It takes me maybe a week and a half, I can't quite tell, but I get to my feet. Lt. Systrom relieves me of the rifle. He nods at me and slits out a faint smile.

"Go have a shower," he says.

I salute. He salutes. And we turn and walk side by side back to the *Benewah*. He even walks a lot closer to me than you would expect.

CHAPTER EIGHT

Slingshot

For the first time since I arrived a month ago, the *Benewah* is behaving like an honest-to-goodness sailing vessel. We are moving upriver.

The days had become a frustrating, repetitive slog of patrols to find and cut supply lines and harass the Vietcong whenever we could flush them out. More and more we found ourselves working alongside regulars of the ARVN, which is the South Vietnamese army. We exchanged gunfire with the enemy once or twice a week without ever really getting close enough to see what we were achieving. But then we would come back the next day and the next week and we would find pretty much the same number of nests of fighters, the same number of listening stations and ammo dumps both full and empty, and one day looked exactly the same as the other in terms of accomplishing anything.

Which is why we are moving.

We have been handing over more of the responsibilities to the ARVN, because a program called Vietnamization is supposed to win this thing more quickly. I don't know. I know that if some guys from some other country came in and told me they were going to *Americanize* America, I would get a little confused. Before knocking all their teeth out.

Maybe, I don't know, but maybe this has something to do with the way our allies are looking at us a little funny, and we are doing the same to them now.

"I won't miss it, that's for sure," Lightfoot says as we sit up on deck watching the riverbanks slip by. "Vung Tau and all that lower Mekong business just felt like a big waste of time and resources. Soon as you sweep an area, it's infiltrated all over again. I'm glad to be headed north. Get closer to the source of all that insurgent activity and maybe have a chance to do something about it. Personally, I wish they would send us right up the whole Ho Chi Minh Trail, get the bull right by the horns."

The Ho Chi Minh Trail is a path cut through the jungle all the way down from Laos, through Cambodia, and right down almost to the capital, Saigon, here deep in the south of the South. It is how most of the supplies come from North Vietnam to the Vietcong.

"It'll be nice to feel like we're getting something done, that's for sure," I say.

"Exactly. And the ARVN — I just don't know about those guys. The longer we were there, the more I felt like they couldn't care less which way this thing went. That was exhausting, as far as I was concerned."

We start walking around the deck of the big tub. It is really a hulk of a thing, with its massive cannons and .30- and .50-caliber machine guns, its crane tower and gigantic helicopter pad like a bull's-eye set right in the middle of it. It's kind of like all the different pieces of the war machinery all grafted together, self-propelled and floating toward the action.

The action now is something called Operation Giant Slingshot. Those very enemy supply lines from the North that Lightfoot mentions have been crazy successful at keeping the insurgents too hot to handle all the way to within about thirty miles of Saigon. We're being sent up there to cut it off and kill it dead, and we are assured that the sleepy part of the war is over for us.

"Body counts," Lightfoot says as he waves to a flotilla of sampans passing by. They are simple low boats that the locals in their triangular hats use to transport *everything.* Some of them are probably carrying guns to kill us with, I can never tell. Lightfoot gives them all a big happy smile with his wave. Nobody responds. "That's what they want now, in terms of progress reports. Body counts. We are going into that jungle, young shooter, and we are going to shoot the daylights out."

"Yes, sir," I say.

"Yes, sir," he repeats, though with the same enthusiasm as he put into that fake smile. "That's one reason you're getting to be the teacher's pet. Lieutenant's looking forward to you picking off a lot of scalps for us. That'll make the unit look good."

"Great. I'm looking forward to that myself."

"That's nice."

I stop looking at Vietnam for a second and turn to the corporal. Despite what he says about me being Systrom's pet project, the truth is that Lightfoot is the one who has taken me under his wing. He is the reason I know anything at all about this place and what we are doing.

"What's it like?" I ask him as he continues to stare off.

"What's what like?" he says, the smile for real this time since he knows full well what I mean.

"Killing a guy. I haven't done it yet. Not that I know of, anyway. You've been in-country what, six months already?"

"One hundred and eighty-one days. DERUS, one hundred and eighty-four days from today."

DERUS. Date Eligible for Return to US. It is a topic of .constant conversation among the guys in-country. This is the first time I have heard Lightfoot mention his.

"Not that you're counting."

"Not that I'm counting. And I had counted all of *three* of them when I first killed a man for certain. We were out on one of those same old patrols. It was getting near dark, and I swear I nearly stepped on this guy hiding under brush. He popped up, and I was carrying the M-60 machine gun that day, and boy was I glad. I was so scared witless I just pulled on that trigger and squeezed and screamed and fired from, like, three feet away, I fired about a million bullets into this poor sonofagun, all straight into his belly.

"I was shaking so much when I stopped you would've thought I was doing some kind of celebration, with both hands on the gun, like an uncontrollable war dance, victory dance, something. I walked up to him and his whole middle was just soup, man. Then his foot twitched.

"And I went into the whole lollapalooza all over again, screaming and shooting and pouring all the rest of the bullets I had into him, into his head this time, until his head just wasn't even a head anymore."

It almost feels, as we stand there not talking now, as if we are actually letting the smoke clear from the shooting, as if it has all just happened all over again here before both our eyes and it's settling again before we speak further.

"So," he says, turning and patting me loudly on the chest with his flat hand, "that's what it's like."

He leaves his hand there on my chest, and I wish he wouldn't. Because I know there is no way he can help but feel the hammer of my heart, and I feel like a kid, stupid and weak and embarrassed.

"Good," he says to me then.

"Good?"

"Good. I was hoping to feel you had one of those in there. Do me a favor. Look after it."

It seems to me to be pretty basic common sense, so I don't feel any need not to grant his request.

"I will," I say. "I will look after it."

He smiles, satisfied, just a tiny bit nutty. "You like cribbage?"

We are belowdecks now, sitting on my bunk, which the Navy calls a rack but I will call a bunk, because this boat is green. He pulls down his cribbage board, and as he sets it up he throws a little bit more light where there was none before.

"It helps if you have some clear idea of who you are killing, and why," he says.

"Makes sense," I say.

"Like I was saying, I never got the feeling I knew where I stood with the ARVN guys. I've heard stories that you would be fighting alongside some of these guys in the afternoon, training them, arming them, and whatnot. And then in the night some of these same guys will have changed their clothes and taken your training and bullets and pumped it all into one of our boys."

He shakes his head, screws up his eyes, as if he is experiencing the confusion and frustration fresh.

"I want to know who my friends are, especially in a

place as crazy and lethal as this. I never felt like the ARVN were our friends."

"Not like the Montagnards," I say, like I really know anything.

He looks up across the cribbage board. He puts his finger on his nose and squashes it down a bit. "The People," he says, almost beaming.

"So, who *are* they?" I ask.

"The term itself means *mountain people*, but it refers to a number of different indigenous tribes of the Central Highlands. Those poor guys we found in the barrel were unusual in that they usually don't come down to the lowlands. But because they are active along the same trails as the communists, and because the Montagnards are siding with us in fighting the communists . . . well, they got on the wrong path somewhere. Either they came too far down in tracking somebody or they got dragged down here as a message, but either way they paid the price for being in the game with us."

"Okay," I say, "so why do they even bother siding with us?"

"Well, truth is, they have a history of not being treated very well by any Vietnamese, North or South. They are a minority people, pushed around, herded up into smaller and smaller pieces of country, getting their land stolen for coffee plantations, shoved aside to live in pens, hilltop reservations. The Vietnamese majority mostly consider them savages. In the end, I think they're mostly doing their best to defend their own reservations against anybody who threatens them. Sound like anybody we know?"

I look at him, thinking about my dad's stories of the Indian Wars, his tattoo, his founding fathers artwork.

"You never told me what your tribe was," I say.

"Cheyenne," he says with clear pride. "And just like the Montagnards, not warriors to be messed with."

"I'll keep that in mind. In both cases."

He is staring at the game now, the board, the score, and my cards. "Do you even know *how* to play cribbage, or are you just being sociable?"

The difference now is: engagement.

The *Benewah* is anchored in the Mobile Riverine Base on the My Tho River, not far from Dong Tam. Traffic of all kinds is a constant now, and we learn to sleep through a city-that-never-sleeps atmosphere, patrols leaving the vessel at all hours and helicopters plunking down and taking off from our roof like we are a commercial airport.

The enemy, bolder than I ever imagined possible, is taking the fight to us in ways big and small and always unsettling.

It is just after midnight, and I hear a great fuss on the deck just straight above my sleeping quarters; then, a few seconds later, I hear a whole lot more below.

Bu-hooom-suplash . . . bu-hoom-suplash . . .

I run up top to see what's happening and find a whole lot of guys wondering the same thing, though probably nine hundred more are sleeping right through it or just not bothering to come up.

"There." An officer is pointing to what may be movement in the water fifty yards away. Four different Navy shooters open fire at the spot for about thirty seconds before the officer calls them off. Echoes and smoke settle down as we all listen for what comes next. But nothing does.

"Buddy, what was that?" I say to one of the shooters.

"Sappers, man. Sappers, right here." He points over the side to the hull of our vessel, just about midship — just about directly south of my sleeping quarters. "We heard the clanging just in time. The sneaky devils attaching explosives to the side of the ship. We got 'em, though, I'm sure of that."

I am only partly reassured.

"You sure you got 'em?"

"Didn't I just say I'm sure? I think I just said I'm sure." He raises his night-vision binoculars, kind of dismissing my rude questioning of his Navy competence. "Bodies'll turn up, don't worry. Why don't you just go belowdecks and lay your sleepy Army head back down and we'll protect you, all right? Have a nice sleep."

I'm sure all the enemy look dead through Navy-colored lenses. I go away, but I don't plan on a *nice* sleep. Which is good, because I don't sleep too well the rest of the night.

Or the one after. I hear things under the deck, under the boat, under the water. And where did all these mosquitoes come from? Jeez, there are billions of them. Relentless little monsters.

"Slap more quietly," Kuns says from a few bunks away.

"Sorry," I say.

I hear something. No, I don't. My hearing has become more acute since I have been in-country, I am certain of that. Maybe too acute.

Clink, clank.

I am not hearing things. I am *hearing* things.

I can't sleep, and anyway, I have to be up for patrol in another hour. I get up, dress, and head topside. There is a sentry with his rifle trained over the side when I get there midship, around the same spot as the other night. He is focused hard, like a hunting dog, on a spot near the bank.

"Something?" I whisper.

"Think so," he whispers. He takes binoculars from

around his neck, hands them to me, and I scan the same area as him.

"Is that . . . are those . . . oxygen tanks? I see a swimmer with tanks on his back swimming this way," I say. The swimmer appears to have something missile-like, about a foot and a half long, in each hand as he kicks toward us.

"That's what I thought," he says, and opens fire.

His first shot pops into the water with a big splash. Then a second, then a third. The swimmer goes under. Possibly. I don't see him. Then I think I do. His hands are empty now, I think. Then I don't see him again.

Three more sentries come running up. Two break out grenade launchers and pepper the spot, big splashes geysering up with the explosions, but who knows what's being achieved.

The firing stops, the smoke and sounds again settle. The officer in charge wearily orders for divers to suit up and examine the hull. Again.

We are walking straight into it on a regular basis, engagement, and we know it. That is precisely what we are here to do, and the adrenaline level is so high I can hear the whistling and wailing from inside my ears almost as loud as the frequent artillery exchanges I hear all around me.

The enemy has been making a pretty good living here out of locating and inhabiting all the best places for ambush. The Brown Water Navy vessels that now buzz up and down the river are constantly under attack from these outposts. Rockets and grenades, machine-gun and rifle fire rain down from elevated spots in the jungle, making life hell for everybody.

Sniffing these guys out and snuffing them out — that's our job now.

Body count counts. I know I have killed men now. I don't know it, but I know it. I keep going out on patrol, and I keep coming back, so I know I am winning. Sometimes we see bodies, or parts of bodies, after we have conducted an assault — sometimes when we haven't conducted one yet. Lt. Systrom counts these bodies as ours. Even a part of a body is a body, four body parts counting as four bodies even if they may have belonged to the same body once. *Disconnectivity* is what he calls it, meaning if they ain't touching, we get to count them all.

"I don't agree with the way they have decided to keep score," Systrom says to me as he takes his knife and cuts the trigger finger off a dead VC. They are his thing, trigger fingers. "But if there is a score being kept, we will score highest."

We are marching, silent marching, which is a brand-new skill I have mastered, up an incline into ever denser jungle. Supposedly, we are working a trail, though there is nothing here you could really call a trail other than a barely discernible parting of trees. The map, though, says it is a trail and that it is hot. There may be insurgents up at the top, or six feet in front of us. It is the height of day in crushing, brutal sunshine, but here under the canopy it is a constant damp dusk. We have been making our way up this parting since just after daybreak. My muscles have all been in a permanent clench the whole time, and my eyes have been strafing the area without a break, like the searchlights that switchback over the sky looking for hostile aircraft. If we were standing toe-to-toe with these guys, bare-knuckle fighting them all day long, it would not be more physically exhausting than this.

I am paired with the lieutenant today, peeling off from the other guys so we can take an overseer's position on higher ground than the main trail. We hike for about twenty minutes when he notices what looks like a nest in the top of a big palm.

"Perfect," he says.

We shinny up the tree, hugging and scrambling and clawing up the forty feet to the highest point in the area. Once up, I am shocked at how right the lieutenant was. I feel we can see all of Southeast Asia from this spot, and the nestlike arrangement of the giant fronds allows enough space for a proper sniper's lie-down, with the second lookout seated upright.

"Wow," I say, taking in the full three-sixty of it.

"Get down, soldier," he growls.

"Yes, sir," I answer, quickly squatting on my haunches.

"I mean all the way down, private."

He holds the M-21 Sniper Weapon System out to me, and I try not to jump up and down. He takes my rifle and the binoculars he had given me before we set out. As I settle into the nest lying down, setting out the bipod legs of the rifle, Lt. Systrom takes his position crouched on one knee, scanning the area through the binocs.

We hear things. There are occasional bursts of gunfire — no shortage of engagements far away and on the river. I hear, not too distant, the now familiar *whoosh* of the flamethrowers off the Zippo boats. There has been a serious escalation in napalm activity, burning away the natural camouflage that's been letting the enemy attack our boats so effectively. The heat coming off the river from that napalm travels back through the jungle and right up the tree to us as if we had ordered air service straight from hell itself. On top of that, we are no longer protected by foliage, so the insane Vietnam sun is pounding our backs, right through helmets and fatigues and equipment like we were no more than fat fish in a frying pan.

"See anything?" Systrom asks me after a full hour of stillness.

I say nothing. I keep my focus through the amazing scope that brings everything on the ground right up into the tree with us.

I can feel my back doing a weird alternating thing. It's drenched with sweat now. Now it's baked crispy dry. Now it is sopping again.

Until I feel it less. I feel my eye, dry, eye, my eye . . .

My eye is in the jungle now. I am attached to the gun by my eye, and together we hover somewhere in the atmosphere between treetop canopy and leaf-litter soft ground. There is a movement here, there, some animal activity maybe, some VC maybe. But nothing in this jungle happens now without my noticing.

Moving bushes are the thing we look for. Bushes that are suddenly in a spot away from where they were a minute ago, and I swear, I swear, I see one now.

It moves. It is not a breeze, a hallucination, or a tiger. It moves again.

I do not say a thing. I watch the bush. It moves again, stepping closer in our direction. It is one person, I am certain of it, though there must be others nearby.

A firefight. M-16 rifle fire explodes in the distance, joined by the machine guns, the grenades, as our guys engage about a half klick north of us. I feel Systrom shift next to me, training the binoculars on the area of the shooting. The distinctive snap of the enemy's AK-47 fire is clear in return. And there is a lot of it.

"I am going to need that weapon," he says while still focused into the distance.

I *need it*, I'm thinking. *I need it more than you possibly could.*

I see him.

A small piece of the moving bush opens, and clear as lightning I see the barrel of the rifle; I see, even, the scope on the barrel of the rifle and the shooter's face pressed into it.

Snap-crack, he gets off his shot.

The bullet whistles straight out and up, right past me, and I hear the small crash and the lieutenant's curse as the binoculars fall from his hand onto my back.

I see him. I see him.

It is four hundred yards, but it might as well be the dry stone wall at the back of the yard at the cabin in New Hampshire. He might as well be a raccoon.

I don't feel a thing. I am aware of squeezing the trigger, but this beautiful thing, so precise, so perfectly balanced and engineered and conceived, does not offer any resistance to my trigger finger. Nothing, no recoil, no bump. I don't feel like I have bones at all.

The scope offers me a view like a movie screen, only with twenty million times the clarity. I see the instant the shot hits the left-center of the man's forehead and throws him backward. I see the chunk of his head, face, temple, skull, whatever, fly off.

"I killed him, sir," I say, trying to be cool, be a soldier, be a man for goodness' sake. I think I might be failing, but I try and I try again. "Got him, Lieutenant Systrom. I got him for certain. I can still see . . ." And I can, because I will not be relinquishing this spot with this site on this gun until someone absolutely insists.

He puts his hand on my shoulder.

Now I have bones.

I feel a very low-level tremor all the way through my body, and I feel it only because I can feel the lieutenant's feeling it. But it is not fear or nerves or shock or anything stupid like that.

It is thrill. It is adrenaline mixed with a shot of *absolutely*, and a bit more of let's-do-this-again pride.

"Well done," he says calmly, but with some satisfaction that I can definitely hear.

"I will take that rifle now, private," he says.

I am this close to answering *oh, no you won't*, even though that would get me a one-way ticket to military jail, but that is simply how huge I feel right now.

But I roll over on my back, straight out as if I am standing at attention horizontally. I present the rifle normally, with two hands, to my boss.

In exchange, he hands me down the binoculars. "Here ya go, have a look through those."

I do. I hold them up to my eyes. I hold what's left of them up to my eyes, that is. The left telescopic tube is just as it was, and through it I see the blazing southern sky. The right tube has been shot in half, the far end of it gone off with the rifle shot, and the whole remaining piece of kit hangs together wobbly.

I have hardly even noticed the raging firefight our guys are involved in, which is continuing right now. But just beyond Systrom I stare with one eye through the solo binoc as one, then two massive helicopter gunships thunder past, heading right for the action. I roll over on my side, the lieutenant crouching beside me, as the gunships fly in low and hard, firing rockets and an impossible barrage of machine-gun fire into the area of the fight.

"I hope they don't hit any of ours," he says low. "For goodness' sake, get that fat head down, Kuns. . . ."

We are down at the base of the tree when Systrom's radio crackles to life.

"Yeah," he says, "is everybody okay? Great. Right. Bring it in."

He gives them the coordinates where we are to rendezvous, and we make our way across the sweaty four hundred yards of brush. I move through the jungle with the softness and silence of a big cat, and my feet do not feel any earth underneath. I am struggling with what I am feeling and trying to understand it at the same time.

How can I be so electro-charged on the inside, so full of rocket power, and at the same time be showing nothing but complete composure on the outside?

I notice Lt. Systrom checking me every few seconds out of the corner of his eye.

"You all right?" he whispers, an uncertain smile creasing his mouth.

I nod, silently padding across the soft ground toward our destination.

He nods in return.

It takes longer to cross the four football fields of distance than it would take to run a five-kilometer race in the real world. But we make it with all our body parts and life force intact, so it is worth the care.

Which is much, much more than we can say for this guy.

Lt. Systrom crouches right down, stopping for no niceties. He takes the rifle away from the enemy sniper, even though it isn't half the weapon the one he's holding is. Then he pulls the body by the leg out of the remaining cover he is in. Once he's got him in this small space of clearing, Systrom takes his hand roughly, like a tough old schoolteacher about to administer a few crisp lashings across the knuckles.

But that's not what he has planned for these knuckles.

I look at the Vietcong soldier, lying there, the top left quadrant of his forehead opened up like a little door off its hinges showing the whole pulp of the inside of his head.

I follow the line of shot, from where we were to where we are to where he is, to where a part of him isn't.

I take three strides toward his flimsy, stupid little bush cover that wasn't ever going to save him from me. I drop down on hands and knees, see the blood, fish around with my hands.

And pull out the hunk of head.

It is the size of the shell off a decent steamed clam.

When I think this, my whole body, for one second, aches for Massachusetts and a bowl of steamers and a Moxie or six.

I stare at the clamshell, then at the former owner. The shell fits exactly, perfectly, in my palm.

"In body-count terms," Systrom says, "now he's a two-score."

I look up when the other guys, Parrish and Lightfoot and Kuns and Arguello, come trooping, silent and stooped and sweaty but unmarked, into our cozy clearing.

Quickly, neatly, respectfully, I take the shell and rub it firmly along my thigh, cleaning up the stray bits and the wet bits as well as I can until it is not clean but clean enough for a person to carry.

I hold it between my hands, prayerlike, and I bow to the dead warrior.

Then I slip the fragment of him into my breast pocket and we begin the march back, two by two.

There is a slap at my back, Cpl. Lightfoot, I believe, but I do not acknowledge it because that would be out of order just now.

CHAPTER NINE

Spirit

"There's a cease-fire," says the voice in my ear.

I leap up out of bed and find Lightfoot. I am not even sure what I am feeling, other than utter shock at the news because nobody, anywhere, has spoken of anything other than war, followed by war, followed by some more war for the foreseeable future. Which was fine by me.

He is laughing in my face, holding me by the shoulders.

"It's just for today," he says.

I fall back down onto my bunk.

"It's for the holiday. Buddha's birthday."

"You're kidding."

"I am not kidding. Both sides have declared a cease-fire, twenty-four hours, from 0600 this morning until 0600 tomorrow. That means we have only twenty-three hours of peacetime left."

"To do what?" I say, reaching under my bed to pull out one of my four remaining cans of Moxie. When the commissary guy finally brought the six-pack out to me, I had to wipe about a half inch of dust off the tops because, he said, nobody ever asks for it. That doesn't make any sense to me, but he did say if he was going to order any more he wanted the money in advance and an extra buck for his troubles. So I guess he meant it.

"How can you drink that stuff?"

"In the morning, you mean," I say through an ecstasy of Moxie burp bubbles.

"Or the afternoon, or when you are conscious, or on any day that has a Y in it . . ."

"Because it is the beverage of the gods," I tell him. "Because it is my strength, my power, my genius."

Lightfoot stares at me, clueless. I feel sorry for the guy.

"Right," he says, "so we got leave. They're just keeping a skeleton crew on duty today, giving the rest of us lucky slobs the day off."

"Cool," I say. "Think I'll go out to the firing range for a load of extra — what are you shaking your head at?"

"I am shaking my head at the most boring killing machine in the whole Army, that's what. I have a better plan for you."

"Yeah?" I say. "What's that?"

"Commemorate," he says sagely, standing right over me with his hands on his hips.

"What?" I laugh, sipping some more. "Commemorate what, exactly?"

"Commemorate *you*, Private Ivan Bucyk. The fact that you broke on through to the other side."

"Other side of what?"

"Of the whole population of the world. There are those who know not and never will know the sensation of the human kill. And then there is us. The vast minority. We who know the righteous kill."

It was righteous. It was right, and it was righteous, and the moment of it has come through the cinema of my mind about a hundred and thirty thousand times just like it is doing right now.

"Do I need to commemorate it?" I ask. "I feel like I already commemorated it. A lot. And like I'm gonna keep on commemorating it for the rest of my life."

"Think of it like this. Catholic, right? Did you get a confirmation?"

"Yeah."

"Okay, it's like that. *Soldier of God* or whatever they called you then. Now you are a soldier of soldiers."

He is very serious about this.

I swing my legs back over and to the floor.

"Okay, so how do you commemorate your first kill?"

"Why, with a tattoo, of course."

Now I show him a little surprise, though I don't like to do that ordinarily.

"What? I mean . . . what? You want me to get a tattoo? That's your big idea?"

"Yes. We all got 'em."

"What? No you don't. I've seen Systrom's, and Arguello's . . . and *you* don't have one."

"Of course I do."

He unbuttons his shirt all the way. He spreads the shirt like the curtains opening on a show. Underneath, he is wearing a tank-top-style undershirt, just like always. He starts squawking a kind of unveiling music.

"You sing like a goose, man," I say.

"Shut up," he says, and raises the T-shirt to his chin. "Ta-dah."

It is, to me, the nicest tattoo I have seen. It is a picture of an Indian warrior nearly naked and sitting bareback on a horse. The horse is standing tall and straight but its ears are back a bit, angry. The brave — long hair falling over his shoulders — is looking up at the sky with his arms spread out at his sides at a forty-five-degree angle to the ground. His palms are up.

"*Appeal to the Great Spirit* is what it's called," he says, all modesty and reverence now. "I got it from a sculpture I saw."

"It's amazing," I say.

The warrior's head is right in the middle of Lightfoot's sternum, the arms stretching out below each pectoral across his ribs. The horse looks to be standing on the corporal's belt.

It is perfectly designed to fit right inside that tank-top undershirt.

"I can't believe I never saw that before now," I say. "I suppose that's why you are about the only guy who never goes around with no shirt on."

"Don't get me wrong," Lightfoot stresses. "I am proud of this. I think it's beautiful. I take it out every once in a while. It's just that whatever I do here, in this place, is between me and the Great Spirit."

I nod. I am staring maybe too intensely at the guy's torso, but I would pretty much defy anybody not to at this moment.

"So you got it after your first kill?" I say.

"Yeah," he says. "It's what we do."

"Can I touch it?" I ask.

"What do you think, it's got texture or something? No, you can't touch it. Get one of your own, then you can go touch it all you want."

He pulls down his shirt, and I pull on my boots.

"I'm not a big tattoo guy," I say, "even though I like my dad's."

"I'm not a big tattoo guy myself," he says, placing a hand on his diaphragm, "but I like knowing this one is here. Makes me believe myself. If that makes sense to you."

I think on it, maybe a few seconds too long.

"Never mind," he says. "It will. Just let's get going."

I don't like writing letters. I don't much enjoy talking on the phone, either, even when the phone is normal and clear and not crackling with static and storms and gunfire and screaming.

I had one of those conversations with Morris. Because he is a radioman now. And he called me. It was okay. Didn't feel like a conversation, like really talking to the guy. But it was okay.

He is right here. *Right here*, with me, somewhere. He is part of Operation Giant Slingshot after getting himself transferred to a Zippo boat in the Brown Water Navy. Before that, he was part of Operation Cocoa Butter out there on the USS *Boston*, floating off the coast, working on his tan and eating pineapple chunks with toothpicks. That's how I pictured it, anyway.

The thing is with Morris, is that contrary to what you would think, a little communication doesn't satisfy him for a while, which it certainly does me. No, a little communication makes Morris need more communication. Right away.

I have a letter.

Hey there Ivanhoe,

Are you okay? It was great talking to you, but you sounded kind of funny. I know the line was awful and all, but, you didn't sound like you. Not that you should sound like you here, since this insanity probably made me sound like anything but the real old me. But you, I figured that this business would make you sound even more like you than ever.

You'll be happy to know they have me shooting guns now. A lot. Much more fighting for me now compared to when I was on the Boston. I don't like it. But I guess I don't hate it. Stop laughing. I see what you mean — a little bit. About what shooting a gun feels like. It sort of settles things? Solves things? I don't know, but sometimes blasting away is a help to a guy around here, and jeez there is a lot of the time that a guy needs it. Mobile Riverine Force is, in a word, NUTS.

Counting that DERUS yet? Oh yes indeed.

Write, man. And I'll keep trying to reach you on the radio.

Morris

I do hate writing.

Out comes my letter to Morris that I have been working on, almost since I arrived on the *Benewah*.

RIGHT, MORRIS. I AM NOT IVANHOE. BUT I DO SEEM TO HAVE ACQUIRED A NICKNAME. THEY ARE CALLING ME MOXIE NOW.

NOT TOO SHABBY, HUH? THE GUYS FIGURED OUT HOW MUCH I LIKE THE STUFF, AND HOW IT IS THE SECRET TO MY SUPERPOWERS AND EVERYTHING. MAYBE IT WAS THE TATTOO THAT GAVE IT AWAY.

SORRY, DID I FORGET TO TELL YOU ABOUT MY TATTOO? THERE IS A TRADITION IN MY UNIT WHERE A GUY'S FIRST CONFIRMED KILL IS CAUSE FOR COMMEMORATION, WHICH MEANS A TATTOO. WHEN IT WAS MY TIME, I HAD NEVER REALLY THOUGHT ABOUT A TATTOO, BUT I WAS HEADING INTO THE PLACE AND I HAD A CAN OF THE STUFF IN EACH HAND. NO IDEA WHAT I WANTED TO GET, BUT I HAD TO GET SOMETHING. THEN I SWIGGED, CRUSHED THE CAN, LOOKED AT THE LOGO IN MY HAND, YOU KNOW, WITH THAT CRAZY-LOOKING SCIENTIST MOXIE GUY STARING AT YOU AND SMILING LOONY AND POINTING AT YOU AND INSISTING YOU HAVE TO DRINK A CAN OF MOXIE RIGHT NOW AND PRACTICALLY JUMPING RIGHT OUT OF THE PICTURE AT YOU? I LOVE THAT GUY.

WELL, IT WAS LIKE A RELIGIOUS THING. I JUST KNEW. IT WAS TOO RIGHT. AND I GOT IT ON MY ARM, ON MY RIGHT BICEP. ONLY. NOT LIKE EVERY OTHER GOON, I DECIDED TO GET IT ON THE INSIDE OF MY BICEP.

HURT LIKE THE DEVIL, BUT ALL MY GUYS WERE IMPRESSED. AND I ONLY HAVE TO FLASH THE TATTOO

WHEN I FEEL LIKE IT. AND I FIGURE, IT'S BETWEEN ME AND MY MOXIE ANYWAY.

HAVE YOU BEEN TO SAIGON? GOT MY TATTOO THERE. IT'S LIKE IF YOU SMASHED UP BOSTON'S CHINATOWN AND THE COMBAT ZONE AND JAMAICA PLAIN AND NANTASKET ALL TOGETHER, ONLY WITH MORE BIKES.

RUDI'S DOING GREAT, ISN'T HE? I HAVE NO REASON TO FEEL GUILTY WITH THE WAY HE'S GOING.

MOXIE. THAT'S ME.

The letter is tucked away again, safe until I can finish it later.

I have heard from Beck. Beck has not heard from me. We are both okay with that because of this main thing that you can say about Beck and me: We are opposites in almost every way except for the fact that we can get along without anybody's support just fine for as long as we need to. If we don't speak until the end of our enlistments, me and Beck will pick up as if four years and yesterday were about the same thing.

I have heard from Rudi, once in a letter where he sounded just like you would expect — scattered and battered and shattered. Then, again, when he was different. He was a lot of different in a little time. Well done, Marine Corps.

I have another letter from Rudi. When did he learn to write so much? Nobody needs this much communication. I have a job to do, and no time to be sitting around gabbing back and forth with other guys who have the same job to do — so get on with it. I am happy that he is doing well, and that nobody needs to feel sorry or scared or guilty for Rudi anymore but, you know, just the presence of the letter right there in front of me, in Rudi's underwater handwriting, is enough of an indicator that everything is fine, and so there's no big hurry to read what he has to say about it just yet, right?

I put Rudi's letter unopened in the footlocker with Morris's unsent letter so they can have a conversation together and keep each other company until I have the spare time to deal with them.

CHAPTER TEN

Free-Fire Zone

The war is taking on a less definite shape, I'm noticing. We have moved farther up the Mekong geographically to where the Cambodian border is close enough you could hear the change of languages if you listened hard. We have been part of IV Corps, then III Corps. We are Army, of course, but paired with the Navy in the Riverine Force. We are part of Operation Giant Slingshot, but when our skills are required, we are joined with or loaned out to or shoved up into another force, another operation, another brilliant offensive.

The big, bright event that established the current tone of things for all of us was the Tet Offensive. That was when the North Vietnamese Army and the Vietcong together targeted all the big cities, the provincial capitals, the important installations of the entire country at the same time. The attacks came on Tet, the equivalent here of the New Year holiday. Who attacks on New Year's, right? Half the ARVN were off on leave, and the rest weren't expecting anything.

That's when it became obvious that there were no borders to this thing. No borders of time and no borders of distance, direction, or determination to do whatever necessary to win.

I was stupid when I came here. I thought the war between the North and the South here was like the American Civil War. There is your North, there is your South, there in the middle is your disputed territory. I thought the North was way up there. I thought either we would push our way all up through South Vietnam and then North Vietnam or maybe they would do the opposite, but it would go one way or the other. Up or down.

I was so stupid. It goes every which way. What's Cambodia got to do with anything, right over there a lot closer to me than any ol' North Vietnam is? But it's teeming with VC, and they come at us from there all the time. Laos. What in the world is Laos? I thought somebody was calling me a name the first time he said that to me, no fooling.

I am not like that anymore, all right? I am no stupid kid anymore.

It is *all* disputed territory. There are enemies in every direction from where I am standing right now. I could get a hole blown through me at any time from anywhere. Because VC are everywhere here and the truth is, most of us GIs couldn't tell you what they looked like if they weren't skulking around at night in their sneaky black pajamas. And now . . . how could they be working so effectively down here, this deep in the South, if people here didn't want them here? Huh?

There is a saying here, from Mao Tse-tung, that goes something like: "The People are the sea that the guerrilla fish swim in."

How do you kill the guerrilla fish without cutting through the sea?

This is one reason for the free-fire zones. I am pleased to hear about the free-fire zones. They help address the chaos.

Free-fire zones are areas where any unidentified person who moves within that area can be considered a hostile and can be dealt with summarily. Things used to be tighter than that. Free-fire zones used to be close around base camps, airfields, and the like.

That was before. That was before we saw how the sea was supporting the guerrilla fish.

Now there are curfews and there are patrols and there are general rules for the people to follow.

Or not. It's up to them.

In the middle of this chaos, I am glad I only have basically one job.

And I get better at it every day.

———————— ★ ————————

Another of the boundaries falling for us is the one between day and night.

When recon comes in with some useful information about the movement of men and equipment along trails, we are on top of it. Sometimes that intelligence says that there is a small block of time, just before dawn or just after sunset, when the enemy is using the path. It is our job to be there well ahead of time, and wait.

This is when the starlight scope becomes the most amazing tool in the whole arsenal: at night. If you need to kill in total darkness from a great distance, the starlight is king. But with the right information you can kill just fine with a number of other tools, usually the trusty M-16 and the M-60 machine gun.

But before you even get to use the tools, you have to be able to use yourself.

"Wake up," Parrish says close to my ear.

I've been sleeping, but that's okay. We are deep into the jungle about two miles inland from the river, split up into teams of two. We have been here all night, in holes we dug ourselves that you couldn't even call foxholes unless you know foxes that stand upright and are about six feet tall. We are only feet from the trail marked off by the recon guys as a highway of VC during the wee, small, darkest hours. We take shifts: one hour sleeping, one hour watching for the enemy.

I hope they come soon, as the hole is filling with seeping, creeping water, like when you dig a hole out on a sandbar at low tide.

Only the sandbar wouldn't have leeches.

"You want me to get that?" Parrish asks calmly.

"If you don't mind," I say, tipping my head away so he can pluck the fat ooze of a creature off my neck. The leeches here are what you would get if you took a normal sea snail, pulled it out of its shell, then force-pumped it full of a half a jar of peanut butter, then put it in the refrigerator for six hours before letting it stick itself to some part of your body.

If only we could turn the mosquitoes on the leeches.

"Don't slap them," he says, angrily whispering. "You can hear a slap for miles. Brush, don't slap."

I brush, and brush and brush. Parrish settles in for his hour.

The other guys are placed twenty yards up and twenty yards back of us along the same trail.

I can feel the sleep of Cpl. Parrish's body against me almost instantly. One thing I am noticing is how tired tired can be here, and how pretty much every soldier I know has developed a knack for going from conscious to un without any in-between time necessary.

I wish I could do that right now.

I am fighting sleep as the night moves toward its conclusion. I am feeling the wetness of my boots, the sloggy dampness of my feet competing with the sweaty dampness of my mosquito-meat face in a game of ultimate grossness in which I am the only loser.

I think, for one of the rare moments I've allowed myself, of home.

You were never supposed to ice-skate on Jamaica Pond. The ice was unreliable, even in the deepest of deep freezes of January and February. You could skate and skate and skate, play some hockey, even, for hours, and everything would be cool, and then *bang*, a long and metal-timber cracking sound would cut right through everything, echo everywhere, and then you would know to turn on the jets and get to the bank.

There was nothing on earth more bone-chilling than sticking an arm into that water through a hole in that ice in the dead-winter months. When the Northeast had been under a relentless coldness and we were bored and stupid enough to have a frozen-arm endurance competition. Layers on layers of clothes just made it worse, the big clunky sweaters, the jackets getting heavier every second 'til it felt like you were hanging in a frozen meat locker and wearing a refrigerator for a sleeve. I always won, of course, but it only took about eight seconds to do so and all afternoon to get feeling back in the hand.

Rudi was never any good at skating. No surprise, really. The other guys were good, I was National Hockey League–level great, but Rudi just never got the hang of it. It was painful to watch him, even, his ankles bent inward in a completely unnatural, inhuman way and somehow carrying all of his weight. He never enjoyed even one minute of it, but he insisted that he was going skating any time we were going, whether it was the legitimate, pay-an-entrance-fee kind of skating at Kelly Rink on the Jamaicaway, or the kind we preferred, which was free and fun and forbidden on the Pond.

Until I couldn't take it anymore, and I banned him entirely from skating. And then he defied me and came the next time anyway, and I was forced to steal his shoes so he had to walk all the way home like a newborn colt with two missing legs, slipping and sliding the whole way and even getting a stress fracture in one ankle.

But he was there again the next time. When we pushed our luck into March, into a freak cold snap that made a St. Patrick's Day skate amid the greenery of the Pond area seem like a perfectly clever idea, Rudi was there. Beck and Morris were there, too, but probably doing pirouettes and stuff near the shore when I dropped through the dead-center ice of the Pond.

"Iv — !"

I only heard the first syllable of the first screaming of my name from Rudi before I went under and the water froze my ears the way scientists turn things to bone china by dipping them in liquid nitrogen.

I fought my way to the surface and heard myself gasp. I was not panicking, not kicking wildly and clawing and flailing like the morons who wind up dead always did. But I wasn't getting anywhere, either. I saw Morris and Beck hurrying over from the far bank. But directly in front of me, Rockin' Rudi barreled my way.

His black snap-buckle overboots were clearly coming undone as he ran with abandon and foolishness, wasting loads of energy on the way.

"Stay away!" I screamed at him.

Slipping and spinning, he put everything he had into ignoring me. Then *bam*, he was down, his cheekbone making a sad pop as it bounced off the ice.

I was trying madly to pull myself up onto the ice, which was crumbling on me like a sheet of milky graham crackers.

"Rudi, man, stop!" I shouted as he got to his feet again. I could see from twenty feet the big pink welt and the panic sitting together on his stupid mug.

Morris and Beck skated up as close as they dared and put the breaks on as sharp as they could.

Rudi had his version of a head of steam up again and disregarded all screams from everyone now as he closed in, took a completely involuntary header, and flew across the ice.

Straight to me.

Straight *into* me.

The top of his capless head banged straight into my nose and I went back under the water. He came under with me, hanging on and following me down a couple feet into the black deep freeze.

Until we stopped short. I kicked and clawed my way, trying for the surface edge and for life, as I felt my strength melting to near uselessness. I felt heavier, colder, weaker than at any other time ever, and I was almost prepared to not do anything more about it. For one of the only times in my life, giving up made a tiny bit of sense.

When a tug, then a tug, then a *heave-ho*, had me breaking the surface of the water like an arctic seal. Bobbing there for a second, I looked to see Morris and Beck sitting on their rear ends, the heels of their skate blades dug into the ice. Each one had a grip on one of Rudi's legs.

Rudi's dumb, drenched face was right in front of me. He looked like he might be crying, even, though I guess his expression had just frozen on whatever stupid thought he'd had when he went under. He'd been dipped into the water from his head to his hips.

After a few more heaves and hos, the team had me out of the water. It took a while as I split the ice like a frozen Moses for about thirty feet before we hit a spot thick enough to hold. We had been in a lot more danger in a lot more thin spots than we'd realized, and that pretty much ended our faith in St. Patrick's help from that time on.

"Thanks," I said as we crawled our way to the safety of the bank. "But, you know, I would have saved myself soon enough anyway. But, y'know, thanks."

"You're welcome," Rudi said with enough beaming pride to make us all toasty warm right there. He was sitting flat on his backside with his paws in front of him, just like a bear does.

"I wasn't talking to you," I said, knee-walking straight over and punching him right in the forehead. It wasn't a real punch, just enough. "That was a really stupid thing to do. When we went under, I was actually trying to drown you. Only reason I didn't was I couldn't figure out how without killing myself at the same time."

He was lying on his back now, staring up at the snowy gray sky and smiling like a simp.

"I don't believe you," he said. "I saved you, Ivan. And I don't feel stupid at all."

I never would have let him get away with that, ordinarily. But it was cold, my hands were stiff, my feet were numb, and it was getting too dark to fight about it.

I am wondering if Rudi would have finally learned to skate right if I'd let him go to Canada, when I notice it's getting too light for the Vietcong to try this trail now.

My feet feel like what I imagine the roots of a mangrove feel like.

"Parrish," I say, waking him up with a gradually building shake. "Corporal Parrish, I don't think there will be any action here today."

He blinks at me about fifty times before it's clear he is back in the land of the living-ish. Over his shoulder, I see Lt. Systrom and Pvt. Arguello trudging our way. As they get near, Lt. Systrom signals to us to get on down the road, back the way we'd come, toward the other guys we will collect along the way.

It takes about a minute, and we stop in our tracks.

Parrish and I simultaneously suck in breath that could bleed all the oxygen out of this whole forest. Arguello just about walks right up my back. Systrom steps around us and walks right up to them.

Cpl. Lightfoot and Pvt. Kuns are still in their hole, semi-upright. Their torsos are forward but their heads are thrown back. Their throats have been cut wide open sometime during the night. It looks like they have huge, gaping mouths, howling or laughing out waterfalls of blood, right in the middle of their necks.

"Don't just stand there," Systrom says calmly.

What a stupid thing to say. Anything else, any other reaction in the whole world, would be the stupid thing to do right now, because just standing here is the exact right and only thing to do.

"Arguello," Systrom snaps, hisses. "Get over here with that radio. Now."

Pvt. Arguello walks, half stooped over, to where the lieutenant is standing, and turns his back to the whole scene. He has the radio mounted on his back. Systrom is calling in details.

"Parrish, Bucyk, get over here," Systrom says between exchanges with the base. "Get them up and taken care of."

We sling our weapons over our backs and slither over there. We drop down, and we each take a fallen comrade.

I grab Lightfoot by his shoulders . . . then I just drop him again when his head bends even farther back. I shake and retch and try again and pull my hands back. I feel like I am tearing farther, actually tearing the flesh of his neck where it is still attached.

Systrom finishes at the radio, shoves me aside, and jumps into the hole with Lightfoot. I roll onto my side and watch as he picks up my friend. Picks him up, cradles him, balances that precarious neck of a very good man in the crook of his left elbow. He talks to him, nose to nose. I don't hear what he is saying. It's between them.

Machine-gun fire explodes all over the jungle, and I can hear the bullets shredding the foliage all around us. We have been ambushed, and it seems to come from every direction.

I leap down to join Systrom in the dead men's hole while Arguello and Parrish haul it back up to the hole I spent the night in. Bullets follow them all the way up until they drop like torpedoes straight down into the ground. Diving headfirst they seem as likely to have broken their necks as gotten shot.

The incoming is so heavy that there's not a chance in the world for us to shoot back. The few times I manage to get the muzzle of my gun and my own muzzle above the lip of the hole, all I can see is a tripling of ricochet, and the bodies of our men jiggering and juddering as they die for us again, again, and again.

The lieutenant had called in the coordinates for helicopters to collect us in the nearest clearing about two klicks away. Even if we could get out of the ground, there is no way we could get there now.

"Corporal Parrish will be calling in the firepower now, private," Systrom says. "You hang in there, and we will be able to wait it out."

"Yes, sir," I say, though I am not too sure about that at all. I have been scared before, and I have been doubtful, but at no point so far in this whole mad mother tea party have I felt what I feel right now, and that is that this is it.

This feels like *it*.

Suddenly, somehow, it all gets worse. Rockets, grenades, beehive shells start exploding all around and I see shrapnel flying right past, like darts embedding themselves in the ground right near us.

Then the throat-choking sound of chopper blades, three, maybe four gunships, and I wonder how all of a sudden our little band of nobodies got so important to the enemy.

"Where'd they get all this firepower?" I ask Systrom desperately.

"It's *ours*," he says, shouting freely now as hell rains all over us. "But it'll kill you just as quick."

And with that, Lt. Systrom shoots up out of the hole, grabs hold of Kuns's shredded, oozing corpse, and pulls it down over himself like a trapdoor spider.

"Sir!" I scream in horror.

"These men are dead, private. Do you wish to join them?"

A large-caliber bullet pumps the earth right by my ear.

I leap up, grab Lightfoot, and stuff him right down on top of me, squeezing him in the process, forcing gasses and fluids out of a hundred punctures, out of him and over me.

The most hellacious firefight I have heard yet rages on above us, as we cling to the lifeless for life and I beg a thousand times over for forgiveness from Lightfoot and his great Great Spirit.

It is, probably, two hours before the only sound we

hear is the choppers. Lt. Systrom and I slowly push our way out, lay the men down yet again, and stand with some difficulty. We walk up to the other hole to check on Parrish and Arguello, and when we near them, we hear Parrish communicating with the choppers. There is no place else for them to collect us, so we still have to make our way to that clearing two kilometers away.

We reach the hole and look down at Parrish, finishing the message, talking from underneath the dead man with the radio on his back.

Three men up, three men down, and a long, heavy walk to the choppers.

CHAPTER ELEVEN

To School

I don't believe in paying any attention to dreams. I don't believe in spirits or spooks or visions or mumbo jumbo of any kind.

Including this. Including mine.

I am looking straight into the face of Cpl. Lightfoot, my friend, which actually did happen, and he is dead, which he actually is.

Then his mouth drops open. We're facing each other, up close, and both of our mouths are wide open because, trust me, if a dead guy's mouth falls open in your face, yours does, too.

There is a breath, a last breath, an escape of the body gasses that build up inside as the tissue starts decaying and whatnot. Not shocking, I guess, medically speaking, but, you know . . . shocking.

But it's the spores. That is what tips it over into another thing, a thing that gets to me more than perhaps a soldier should be gotten to. The breath he puffs out in my direction is visible, like a cloud made up of tiny, tiny droplets of his blood, a mist of his blood, and I gasp, because trust me on this again, when a dead guy breathes up a cloud of blood spore, you gasp.

And so it winds up inside me, doesn't it? I breathed it all in, and I can feel it.

What's that all about?

There are reports all the time. Reports of guys doing their tours, hitting their almighty DERUS dates, and rotating out of here. They arrive back into society some-how unfit for society. Like, nuts beyond nuts, unable to readjust to a place where sneaking around and killing everybody and everything — you should see guys around here when they get turned loose on thickets with a machete — is just not the way things work.

I say, the guys who are loony tunes are the ones who got things exactly right while they were here. If you are here, it makes complete sense. There are, as far as I can tell, three ways guys get through the experience of Vietnam.

You can keep moving. The machine is built so that, if you want to, you can spend your whole twelve months in a state of constant motion, fake-fighting, passing through the war like a disinterested tourist.

You can acknowledge the reality of the situation, real-ize how close you are to horror every single day, and blow your mind out in a frenzy of nonstop nerve-racking.

Or, you can snap it. Like when you snap an ammonia capsule under the nose of a guy who is losing consciousness, and he comes popping out of it like some whole new creature with a whole new look. When you snap it here, you suddenly say, it's not really real at all, not the way they think it is. What is really real is, I am death. I am death walking through this thing, and so I can't possibly die.

Snap.

There is a popular theory floating around, and that is that there are some peoples here, some shaman types indigenous to this land, who curse the head of every American soldier for every single day he is here. The curse says these soldiers will never, ever find peace because of the things they have done here. They will walk the earth as lost, empty souls at war with themselves and everyone else. Ineligible for contentment in this world or any other.

I don't think much of that theory, but there it is.

I am on my belly, on the firing range. The range here is not big enough, but it is a range. With only the M-16, nobody expects to be very accurate much beyond two hundred yards anyway, so this is probably practice enough. I never miss dead center anymore, unless I sneeze or cough. Sometimes I work up a sneeze or a cough to see if I can do it anyway.

"Private Bucyk," comes the voice from above me.

"Yes, sir," I say, squeezing off another shot. I should probably be on my feet by now. But I am shooting.

"On your feet, private."

An order, of course, is another matter. I will always be a soldier.

"Yes, sir, Lieutenant Systrom," I say, at attention now.

The sun is blazing hot, as it always is unless it is chucking down rain. There is a glistening of sweat on the lieutenant, but I am soaked through.

"You know, don't you, that being a sniper is about a lot more than fine shooting."

"Fine shooting is only approximately twenty percent of the job, sir," I say.

He smiles. "Ah, yes, I suppose I have mentioned it a few times. Anyway, yes, it is about stealth, it is about location and stalking and camouflage, independence . . ."

"Nerve, stamina, and transcendence, sir."

"My," he says, shaking his head, "I do talk a lot, don't I?"

"Yes, sir, for a sniper you do, sir."

"All right, all right," he says, waving me to shut it. "What I want to know now is, how interested are you in learning the trade properly, formally?"

I feel my eyes go wide, even as the sun hurts them more.

"Ninth Division is running its own Sniper School

these days, in-country. It's an eighteen-day program, a tough program, fifty percent failure rate. . . ."

"When can I start, sir?"

"Should I take that as you volunteering, Private Bucyk? Because this is strictly for volunteers. I can't force you —"

I do my best to maintain my crisp and official voice, but it is hard.

"Are you toying with me . . . *sir*?"

He nods, shades his eyes from the sun so he can look more properly into mine.

"I will get to work on it and let you know. Meanwhile, how are you holding up?"

"Fine, sir."

"You sure? No lingering . . . ?"

"Corporal Lightfoot was a fine soldier and a fine man," I tell him.

"You don't need to tell me."

"Arguello, and Kuns . . . Kuns hadn't even earned his tattoo yet, sir. Body count was zero. Never even had a chance to —"

"He had every chance, private. Kuns was a *shaker*, you are a *shooter*. Sad as it is, but we are stronger without him."

With that he turns sharply on his heel and marches toward the next thing.

———————— ★ ————————

If Sniper School had a motto, it would have to be, *The Maximum of Death to the Minimum of People.*

My father will be more than proud.

It is the most appropriately spent eighteen days of my life.

When I arrived in Vietnam, I knew a lot about shooting and a little bit about camo and concealment, observation techniques, and the precision skill of estimating the range of a target.

Now? I know almost everything about almost everything. I wear tiger-stripe camouflage gear. And I am personally responsible for one M-21 Sniper Weapon System.

Sometimes the universe and the Army get it exactly right.

"You are now thirty-five thousand times more deadly than you were before," says Major Howell, addressing the graduating class of twenty-one of us.

I like the sound of that.

"Because while the average soldier in the field in this conflict fires fifty thousand rounds per kill, the average for the trained sniper such as yourself is 1.39 rounds. Do you know what that means?"

I am going to guess that he isn't going to refer to how cost-effective we are.

"It means, men, that you are going to be very familiar with the concept of intimate killing. When you fire your weapon, a man is most likely going to die. When you get someone in the crosshairs of your sight, at that very instant in time you are going to know that individual, personally, more than anyone else ever will again. It takes a special brand of fighting man to handle that. This ceremony today certifies that each and every one of you is indeed that special kind of fighting man."

Before I was good.

Now I'm *special*.

"Are you okay, Moxie?" Parrish asks as I sit on my bunk, polishing my weapon. Every day at Sniper School, one of the instructors would disassemble the weapon, and we would have to clean and oil it. Then he would put it back together again. We could never do the breakdown or reconstruct. Not until the last three days. I did the whole thing twenty-four times in the last three days. This weapon and I are so intimate, I would bet you that it would come if I whistled. That is, if I ever let it get far enough away that I would need to. Which I don't.

"Of course I'm okay," I say. "I'm more okay than anybody. Want to play some cribbage?"

I pull Lightfoot's cribbage board and the cards out of my footlocker and lay them on the bed. Parrish stares a screwed-up face at it as if I'd just barfed there.

"No, man," he says, but sits down as if the answer was yes, man. "That's a Navy game anyway. That's a *submariners'* game." He says the word *submariners* as if he's got one caught down low in his digestive tract.

"How are you, then?" I ask.

"Not all that terrific, thanks for asking."

Things are different now, since half our team got shredded to cabbage. We don't have the same certainty and regularity we had as a unit. We are still here on the *Benewah*, but it seems like the Riverine identity is taking over a bit, like we have one foot in a green boat and the other in a gray boat and they are drifting different ways until something has to give.

"You know what they got me doing now? I go out every evening on one of those crazy PBRs," Parrish says. PBR stands for Patrol Boat, River, the small craft you see all over the place here. "We do like the name says, and we patrol the river, but more and more it seems to me that we have the primary goal of exposing and soliciting enemy fire for somebody else to go clean out later. We are like one of those carnival shoot 'em games, you know what I mean?"

I know well what he means, and I smile at the thought of Paragon Park. I wonder what I'll score when I get back?

"Man, Bucyk, I'm telling you, we get shot at every *day*. And the boat gets *hit* every day. The sound alone, of the pinging, and the whistling of rocket fire, is enough to put a guy right out of his mind."

"Cribbage?" I say.

"No," he says, "stop that. And it's bad luck to steal board games from dead people. A fortune-teller in Saigon told me that."

"That's funny," I say, pointing at him with one hand and polishing with the other.

"Is it?" he asks, though he is laughing. "I can't tell anymore."

"Listen, you want me to shoot these guys for you?" I say.

"Oh, Bucyk, would you? That's awfully nice of you. Thanks, problem solved."

"There."

"There, what? I do have my own gun, you know. And it's a real something, too. A 105-mm howitzer, baby, an absolute *cannon*. I think when I shoot the thing off, it scares the Navy guys on my own boat more than it does the VC on the banks."

"Great. Then what's your problem?"

"The problem, my man, is that no matter how many times I kill these guys —"

"I am thirty-five thousand times more lethal than you are, by the way, have I told you that?" I say, interrupting with an important and pertinent truth.

He stares at me deadpan.

"I once killed a guy with a cribbage board, have I told you that?"

"I like your moxie," I say.

"Aw, now you're just getting weird, man. Cut it out."

"Please continue with your story."

"No matter how many times I kill these guys, they are all right back there the next day. I mean, *all of 'em*. In the exact same nests, practically, as if to say they are just not bothered by what we are doing at all. I mean, what are we supposed to do about that? I realize I'm a corporal and you're just a private, but come on, you *stink* of Real Army . . . take no offense. . . ."

"Why would I?"

"So, I mean, where do we go from here? What do we do?"

I am preparing to solve this small problem for my friend when the boss comes in. Parrish and I stand at attention. He waves us back down.

"Lieutenant," I say, "any chance I can ride with Parrish and his PBR this evening?"

"None whatsoever, corporal," he says.

"But what if — *corporal*?"

He hands over some stripes. "The first of many field promotions, I imagine. Congratulations, Moxie," he says, and shakes my hand.

Parrish then shakes my hand, too, adding, "Don't get all excited, they're giving these to everybody out here."

"Sir," I say as the lieutenant turns to leave. "Parrish's PBR . . . ?"

"Will have to get along without you. Your orders are to take three days off, after which time you will be reassigned. To some lucky operation that is in dire need of your specific set of skills and, training. Congratulations again, Moxie. You are leaving the madness of the Riverine Assault Force."

My head is swimming as I sit there. I consider all the possibilities.

And I think I like them all.

"What should I do for three days, lieutenant?"

"The beauty of that is, you can decide for yourself. I suggest you bug out, go to Saigon, live a little. Relax, refuel, refresh. Follow your heart, knock yourself out. But if I see you set foot on one single river assault vehicle before you go . . . well, just remember what distance I can pick you off from, soldier."

I smile and nod and force myself not to say that I can now do the same thing from the same distance so I'll wave to you through my starlight scope.

"Excuse me?"

I have wandered where I dared not tread before.

"Corporal Bucyk," I say, saluting though I have no idea what rank the man is or if I don't maybe even outrank him. I don't care. I know what turf I am on and what kind of soldier I am addressing, and in my book he is worthy of a salute.

"Moxie," he says, expressionless. The fact that he knows anything at all about me gives me a greater jolt than finding an enemy, a viper, or a corpse in the jungle. "What do you want?"

"I would like to go out. On operations. With you and your people."

A wide grin opens up across a very partial set of tan-colored teeth with no enamel to them at all.

"You," he says with mock shock, because I am certain he does not know the real kind, "want to be a LRRP?"

"No, sir," I say. "But I have three days before transfer. Lieutenant says to do what I want. This is what I want."

I feel already transformed as I prepare myself for the night. I am wearing my tiger stripes, which almost none of the other Army guys have. I have my face all painted up, the night-fighter cosmetic cream under my eyes to cut the glare from any incendiary action. I have my M-21 sniper rifle, my bandolier of ammo, my pistol, my knife at my side.

As I leave the *Benewah* for probably the last time before I leave it for good, I feel like I could win this thing by myself. I feel like I could take a small detour up the Mekong banks, and before Parrish and his new pals had to deal with any hostiles again I could go up there and see them dead and see that they stayed dead.

There is nothing worse than the feeling you have to kill the same enemy day after day after day.

Unless it is the feeling that you are not really killing him at all. I personally could not sleep with that.

But I don't take any detours, because frankly I can't wait to join up with these guys and get out there.

My man greets me once I cross the base and enter the almost segregated sub-compound of the LRRPs.

"All packed up?" he asks, a formality since he goes right to work pulling apart my knapsack, pockets, everything. "What's this?" he asks, pulling the dried, chipped, and scored disc from my breast pocket.

"That's my good luck VC head bone, sir."

He nods and tucks it back in my pocket. "Everybody should have at least one of those. Listen, call me Makita, right?"

"Right," I say.

He takes all my food and dumps it out right there on the ground. I brought the usual C rations: beans, something meatlike, fruit, peas, tuna.

"Nope," he says, "nope, nope nope," and with each *nope* tosses another can over his shoulder. "Here," he says, handing me back a single can of peaches, "you can keep this."

Though I'd been told that we would plan to be back by morning, you always make provision for an extra day at least. Now I have thoughts of being stranded out there with just my water and one can of peaches.

Makita reaches into his own backpack and starts shoveling compact packets of food into my bag. It's all going too quickly, but I know it is the freeze-dried stuff that takes up less room and weighs less, and is a sort of LRRP perk.

"Most important of all," he says, "this stuff don't make any noise. You don't want to get scalped just because you had to pull the lid off your stew. Our food is quiet food. Except the chili. The beans are like ball bearings, so don't bother chewing or they will hear you in Laos."

Twenty minutes later, we are up in the air. I am tagging after with a team of six grim-faced men covered in war paint and malice. We are chopping through the sky in a helicopter headed north. I see the Mekong running along below us, and it is still light enough that I can make out the traffic of our assault vessels chugging up and down and out to the edges.

Parrish is probably down there, cursing the whole thing.

Morris is probably down there. Morris could well be right *there* and trying to radio me, the big baby.

"What are you pointing at?" Makita asks me.

"Oh," I say. "Didn't realize I was. Just identifying craft. I don't usually get this vantage point. Zippo right there."

He nods, and we watch out the side as we pass over the countryside, and I think what a great carnival ride this could be, swooping low over the treetops where you can smell the green almost as much as the gunpowder and napalm. It's a thrill ride, but maybe not what the average carnivalgoer is looking for.

I am not told where we are going or what we are doing, but I have been told that I will not be told, so I'm okay with it. A need-to-know basis is how Makita sees it.

"And I will let you know if I think there is a point at which you need to know."

Apparently, LRRPs like to remain under deep cover even when they are talking.

"It's a long country, Moxie," he says, still scanning terrain off in the distance. It *is* long, top to bottom, and not all that wide. So while we are down here fighting away in the all-important Mekong Delta, and in all the areas surrounding Saigon and' what's supposed to be the Government of all South Vietnam, well, we are a whole lot closer to other countries than we are to the country we are supposed to be here fighting in the first place.

I am wondering where he is headed with this, but something intuitive tells me not to question a LRRP unnecessarily.

"Folks back home, I think they think this is like the Korean War, you know, as if all these stupid wars in this part of the world are the same as long as one side's a North Something and the other side's a South Something and there are commies involved. Well, it ain't just North versus South here, is it?"

"No, it isn't."

"No, it isn't. It is North versus South, sure. But it's also North versus South and South versus South and South versus everybody, and everybody versus *us* as in US. So the people criticizing what we are doing here haven't got the first clue what's going on. They think we're supposed to be like the Redcoats or something, just standing up in a straight line, walking right up to the other side's straight line, and settling things all neat and up front. Ain't possible. Ain't possible. So we have to do things otherwise. You understand."

"I do, absolutely," I say.

And I do, more or less.

"How's your body count coming along?" he asks matter-of-factly, like I'm building a go-cart in the garage or something.

"It's okay," I say.

"'Cause it's all they care about at this point. That's not good, really. It's not good warfare. Means either the people at the top don't really know how to conduct a successful campaign or that they are giving up on actual progress."

I don't know how far I want to go with this individual into this particular verbal incursion. I am no expert, that is for sure. I shoot people. That's it.

"Well," I say, "I guess they figure as long as we have all these guns . . . and gear for blowing stuff up . . ."

"Ha," he says, as much of a grunt as a laugh.

"I suppose free-fire zones are going to help with that body count thing, eh?" I say.

He turns an entirely quizzical look on me, like I couldn't be serious at this stage of the game.

"They are *all* free-fire zones, Moxie," he says.

I have to try this much. "What about civilians?"

His look, sincerely, goes into a deeper puzzlement. "There are none. Where have you been?"

He holds me with that look, that stare, for several penetrating seconds, waiting to see me through this, to escort me to my senses. I find myself, weirdly, running my fingers up and down my bandolier of ammunition, like I am playing some sort of explosive accordion.

He slaps my leg. "Confirmed kills?"

"Three," I say quickly. "Possibly four."

"Three, then. Oh, you're gonna have to work on that, my man. We have to make our numbers. Don't want to get fired or nothin'. What are you gonna do way out here without a job?"

It is all but impossible to tell whether Makita is joking, enjoying himself, what? And his gallery of mirthless rogues don't give me a clue which way to go, either.

Which makes it extra welcome when we make our descent into a grassy field on the edge of thick forest. All the LRRPs silently move into gear, and I follow the fifth man to the exit.

The chopper barely touches down, as if it is a game of tag rather than a personnel transport. Only two men actually disembark before the skis are back off the ground and headed the other way.

The third man jumps, lands on his feet. Fourth does the same, fifth jumps from a height of eight feet, bounces, rolls smoothly.

I get to the lip when we are about twelve feet up. I hesitate, costing myself another two.

Makita gives me a push, and I see the tall grass waving me in as it rushes right up.

I land just barely on my feet, but falling forward, and hit the ground hard with my chest.

I lie there for a few seconds before Makita grabs me roughly by the back of my shirt, stands me upright on my feet, and shoves me a lot harder this time toward the trees at the tail of the running chain of LRRPs.

We gather once we are somewhat safely inside the tree line. It is so dense here, with triple canopy above and hardly any bare trail in any direction, it is easy to imagine we are the only humans to have been in this spot for five hundred years. If ever.

"Makita," comes a voice from the blackness no more than twenty feet in.

"Yo, Ben," Makita says, opening up a map.

My theory of a primeval forest untouched by man would seem to be flawed.

One LRRP pulls out a machete that looks like it could bring down a sequoia. He begins sharpening it.

There are many things I have learned about men, about combat, and about myself during this portion of my life, and I am learning more daily, probably at a faster rate than I learned things as a toddler. One of the things I am pleased to discover is that fear and uncertainty have the effect of making me more, and not less, bold.

"Do I have a need to know yet?" I ask.

Makita turns from the map he is studying with two other men under a very low flashlight. He shines the light in my face so that I am probably the only thing illuminated for five miles.

"Not sure you have a need yet, strictly. But fair enough, you probably have a right. Maybe. How 'bout we just say we are not in Cambodia. How's that? Because, what with Cambodia being a neutral nation, it would be incorrect for us to be there, no matter how rotten with Vietcong it is.

"That narrow things down for you enough?"

I deep-breathe, in, out, then steady. "That will suffice," I say.

It was made clear to me that I may or may not have a chance to shoot, but that otherwise I would be falling in line and not taking on any of the LRRP responsibilities. I am a hired gun, not a part of this team and not to be in the way.

"If this was 1964, they'd be calling you a *military adviser*," was how Makita put it.

So now, as the men converge on their evening plans, I stare into the blackness, toward the voice, and stare at the mystery.

Eventually, when the LRRPs break from their huddle like an eerily silent NFL offense ready to play, there comes the smallest sound of padding footsteps from out of the forest.

Two men, welterweights in Army green, come straight up to me. They wear sidearms, rifles over their backs, machetes at their waists — armed to the teeth like most of us. They are dark-skinned but not ethnic Vietnamese, that is for sure.

Something bubbles up in me and I feel like a kid again at Fenway or Boston Garden hanging by the gate for autographs.

"Montagnards?" I say.

"*Montagnard* is a French term," the first man says. "But yes. There are many mountain tribes. We are Degar." He extends a hand. "And your tribe?"

"Wow," I say, "this is amazing stuff. How did you know I had American Indian blood?"

"I didn't know that. I was just . . . making introductions."

I already feel pretty stupid. But I get over it quickly, like you do with things here. I actually look over my shoulder to see if there are a bunch of LRRPs laughing at me.

Stupid me. LRRPs don't laugh. They are still deep in planning, going over maps, gesturing silently toward the distance, checking and rechecking weapons that seem to be appearing like mushrooms all over their bodies.

"I'm Ivan," I say. "And if you don't mind my saying so, your English is amazing. Better than about ninety-five percent of the GIs I know."

"Thank you. Most of your people call me Ben. You can call me Ben."

"Thanks, Ben, it's an honor. All I hear about you guys is that you are incredible soldiers, scouts, trackers, and trustworthy allies." I look past him to his partner.

Ben turns to the man and starts speaking to him quickly.

"French?" I say.

"*Oui,*" Ben says to me. "You understand French, yes?"

"Aw, man, naw. Just, you know, Pepe Le Pew stuff, *le mew, le pant, le sigh,* that kind of thing."

Frenchie gives me a quick bow, which I return. When I bow, my bloodied scapular spills out of my shirt. Frenchie is drawn right in. He comes up to me and, blood or no, kisses the Christ image gently before making the sign of the cross. Ben then makes a sign of the cross, and I try not to be in a constant state of surprise here.

"English and French, Chinese, every Montagnard dialect, am I right, Ben?" Makita says over my shoulder.

"More or less," Ben says modestly.

"Don't be shy, man. You are the backbone of our entire Army. Without you we'd all be dead meat."

Ben refuses to even acknowledge that one. "Shall we walk now?" he says.

"We shall," Makita says, and we walk.

And walk.

And machete-slash pathways.

And walk. In single file. For four hours.

When we finally come to an extended stop, we are in a slightly less dense version of the same bush we entered. We are in a semi-open patch that is circular and about twenty feet in diameter. This is where we settle in to sleep for two hours, with half-hour guard duties divided up evenly.

"What happens then?" I ask Makita, not really expecting much but hoping to possibly catch him groggy and less guarded.

He is lying on his back, resting, yes, but staring straight up like a guy who possibly never does truly sleep.

"What does the second R in LRRP stand for, Moxie?"

"Recon."

"Correct. So when we get to our destination, we are gonna recon. We are gonna con, and recon, and re-recon if necessary until the task is complete and it is time to return to base with some priceless intelligence we can pass on up to our good friends at Special Ops."

Special Ops usually follow, where LRRPs blaze a trail.

I stare at him. "Right."

"Does that clarify things for you nicely, then?"

Of course not. "Yes."

"Good night, then."

"Good night."

When I wake up, Ben and Makita are about twenty yards deeper into the woods and a whole lot deeper into planning. They are both making gestures, right, left, and skyward. Ben makes a lot of chopping motions in the air, while Makita favors punching.

And we are off again. This time, though, the walk has a greater intensity, a feel more of marching than trekking. I have seen several if not all of the LRRPs popping their medication out of their shirt pockets. Makita even offered me a few pills. Army medics routinely dispense pills to the nighttime operations guys to keep them awake, sharp, and responsive. Taken in enough quantity, they say it also makes you fearless and furious.

I figured my nap was enough to get me through.

This walk only lasts an hour anyway, before we all find ourselves stationed in a fan formation just before the forest opens up onto a small hilltop village. There are about eight or nine small huts on stilts and nobody visible outside them just now.

Makita has me up a tree, about thirty feet off the ground, where a dividing branch makes a perfect nest. When I set up and lie forward, I can see every hut's front door through my powerful scope.

And as they wake to the new day, I can see the people.

They remind me more of early American Indian tribes than anything. The first activity I see is a number of women, ten, maybe, and twice that many children gathering in the middle of the common area between huts. They carry big jugs and pots, and head for the stream that is visible about a quarter mile to the east of their hilltop. When they have gone, I see the first man, standing in his doorway, making some kind of gesture, prayerlike and rhythmic with bowing toward the sun. He says things to the sun as he does this. He is wearing what is not much more than a loincloth.

If you forgot everything else, you could think you were looking at the high Great Plains of America in 1840.

Makita scurries up the tree to me like a big spider monkey.

"Turns out we do have a use for you after all," he says.

"Who are they?" I ask.

"Them? They are Khmer Loeu. They are kind of like the Cambodian Hill People version of our guys, the Montagnards. Only a lot more primitive, frankly. More to the point, they are the Vietcong's version of our Montagnards."

"Meaning?"

"Meaning, they are partly responsible for a lot of the inexplicable nastiness that's been trickling all the way down the Mekong and into Saigon. They work as scouts and suppliers and gunrunners and quiet assassins for the enemy, and up 'til now we haven't been able to see the sneaky invisible devils, never mind get a hold of 'em. Thanks to our man Ben, we got something big here, Moxie. And here's where you come in. Now that the women and children are out of the way, the LRRPs are heading in. You are to stay right here and scan, eagle eye, the whole site there. And I don't believe it'll be necessary, but as soon — and, Moxie, I mean as *soon* — as you see a single weapon appear on any one of them guys, you do your well-trained assassin thing and put his lights out. You understand me?"

I can see, in the redness of his eyes and the insistent tone of his voice, that his amphetamine and his gung ho are both kicking in and kicking up.

"I understand."

He is perhaps picking up something in my own voice and my own eyes.

"Moxie," he says, hard. "If one of my men gets a hole in him because the overseer wasn't quick on the trigger . . . let's just say it's a long way from home for somebody who officially isn't even here, you get what I'm saying?"

This. This is the moment I am most scared in the whole war. And it is from one of our guys.

"I understand completely," I say.

I train my sight on the village again, going from one hut to another like the world's most seriously unwanted door-to-door salesman. Then I see the Montagnards walking out of the woods, up the side of the hill to the village. The first man out of his house, the sun worshipper, stiffens up and puffs out at the sight of them. But he doesn't move, and he doesn't seem too alarmed.

Ben and Frenchie walk up to the man and begin what looks like a very friendly chat, exchanging the latest mountain talk, as everyone says the various mountain peoples have related better to each other for centuries than they have to the wider culture. I see the man relax his posture a bit, then both Ben and the man gesture a little ways up the hill to the central structure in the middle of the little village.

The three of them walk that way, and the Khmer Loeu man makes some sort of hooting call, bringing other men out and headed to that same structure.

Eventually, the Montagnards and all the men disappear into the communal hut, which must be the central meeting place for the villagers. All the men are dressed much the same, some in the loincloth style, some with army pants or the black pajamas you see on a lot of VC.

But none of them are armed. I relax. A little.

As the last of them disappear into the structure, the amped-up LRRPs spring into action. Single file, they attack that hill with stealth and speed and directness that would make my father and thousands of fighters from the old-time wars cheer with recognition.

In minutes, the LRRPs have all poured into that building and, like a miracle, without a shot and with little collateral fuss, a cell of what I have to assume are dangerous insurgents has been captured.

I haven't done a thing. But a surge of pride takes over

me, and I look to the sky, aiming my rifle at a defense-less cloud for a second before bringing it back down.

On two young villagers. Younger than me. They have just stepped out of that first house and are creep-ing tiptoe toward the big meeting place.

Each one is carrying an American M-16 rifle.

God.

God, no.

There is no no. There can be no no, Ivan. There can be no no.

I bring my M-21 sniper rifle, manhunter, boyhunter, down, get the rear kid straight in the crosshairs, and squeeze. I shoot him right in the back of the head. He falls forward, the gun flying, his face bouncing off the ground.

The second lead boy turns in the direction of the shot. He looks toward me without even properly raising the weapon.

"Raise your weapon, son," I say, hearing a voice say it, then hearing *my* voice say it. "Raise your weapon, son."

And he had more than enough time to raise his weapon, not that it would have done him one tiny bit of good anyway.

I pull the trigger and watch the spray of blood as the round penetrates his young, stupid forehead, and he falls forward, his damaged skull bouncing off his friend's. His brother's? His somebody's?

They were smart boys, too, I'm thinking to myself as I continue to scope them there on the ground. They knew. They knew something was not right. More than the men, who trusted their fellow mountain people so easily. Smart boys. Knew enough to get out of both the meeting *and* the water fetching. Because they were clever enough to get out of all that, and they were boy enough to want to.

And because they were right in the middle, not the kids anymore, and not the men yet.

The procession starts. The Montagnards come stepping with a sense of grim, unflustered purpose, walking right past the bodies, on the way to here, to me, to the trail we cut and will now retrace. Right behind them and even more intense, the six LRRPs come marching in line, each one of them shoving a mountain man who has his elbows tied painfully sharp behind his back and a bruised and bloodied mess on his face.

Two-thirds of the men who went in that structure are not now coming out of it.

Off to my right, in the distance, I see the women and children carrying the water back up the hillside for all the folks of the village.

The parade marches beneath my tree perch and past.

"Thanks," Makita says as he passes, bringing up the rear. His tone is as if this is just another day at the office, another job adequately executed. "You're up to five now."

Confirmed kills. Five now.

"Do they even add up to a whole one together?" I say as he walks on.

That's what I say, to have something to say, but I'm not thinking that.

They add up to about a million, is what I'm thinking.

Nobody says anything about my still being up the tree. Nobody tells me to get a move on or to catch up or indicates that it matters at all whether I make the trip back or not.

CHAPTER TWELVE

Moxie

By the time I eventually reach my bunk again, twenty-seven of my free seventy-two hours have elapsed. By the time I wake up after falling into that bunk, the figure has reached forty-three.

"You stink, corporal," Lt. Systrom says, standing over me.

I can't dispute it. I am lying here in my tiger stripes, in my face paint, my pillow looking like it's about to go out on its own dirty recon op. I reek of a lot of things.

"So this is what you do for fun," he says.

"I suppose so."

"Well, if it's any satisfaction to you, there seems to be a lot of good information coming out of those prisoners who were brought in that you had nothing to do with."

"Information," I say flatly. "Like fashion tips or who's gonna win the big elephant race on Saturday?"

"Ah, don't know about any of that. But we do know how a lot of the American weapons and artillery we have been supplying to our ARVN allies seems to be turning up on the other side. There's nothing we like better than getting killed with our own stuff, Moxie, and there's gonna be a few knocks on a few of our *allies'* doors the next several days."

I sit up on the bed, put my feet on the floor.

"Could get exciting," Systrom says. "You sure you don't maybe want to stick around a bit longer to join in? Could be very satisfying work." He is waving an envelope by his ear.

"No, thanks," I say, taking the envelope from him.

"Well, you are due out tomorrow, but there is a chopper you can be on this evening if you like."

I nod and get up. I go to my footlocker, open it up.

"You'd better get to work cleaning yourself up. I wouldn't let you on my chopper like that, and it looks like it could be an all-day cleanup and pack-up job."

"True," I say, rooting around in the locker. I put the envelope in there and dig for the other one.

He gestures at my orders rolling around now with my socks and shoe polish and whatnot. "Don't you even care where you're going to?" he asks.

I look up from my kneeling position. "No, sir," I say, neither here nor there, but just sayin'.

He looks a little sad, and a lot knowing.

"Yeah," he says, hands on his hips as he turns and leaves. "Yeah."

I find what I am looking for in my footlocker. Well, there is the forever letter I am writing to Morris. I'll get back to that. I stuff that letter and take out the one from Rudi that I haven't even opened yet. I am picturing a page crammed with his lunatic scribblings, on and on and crazy.

PAl,
PAllEST PAl PAl,

    I do NOT have much time Right Now, IVAN, because I NEVER have time lATEly is why. I volUNTEER fOR EVERything, ANd if I did NOT have to slEEP I NEVER would. I slEEP lESS thAN EVER, it's gREAt. I do SO much, I'M likE A wholE wAR.

    ThANKS, is whAt I wANTEd to sAy while I hAd the time. ThANKS. To you. ThANKS, IVAN. You mAdE it, you did it, you mAdE mE. If I didN't do this I would bE Nobody ANd worSE thAN Nobody. I owE you EVERything. You ARE the oNE. Who took thAt thiNg I wAS, ANd mAdE mE bE this. ANd I will NEVER EVER fORgET whAt you did fOR mE.

    I hAVE to go but I will tEll you mORE REAl sooN. But I wANTEd you to KNow. I wANTEd you to bE PROUd of mE.

    I Am NOT A Kid ANymORE, IVAN. I wish I wAS you, but I will NEVER bE you, but I Am NOT A Kid

*ANymoRE, tHAt's foR SuRE, AnD I Know you don't
likE mush At All but, just, tHAnks.*

*tfour tero I mean you are my tero,
RuLi.*
P.S. How much do you love free-fire zones?

I am sitting on my bunk, elbows on knees. My left
hand holds the letter while my right hand squeezes my
face, rubs my face, takes the warrior paint and smudges
it more and more until my face is one great soup of camouflage grease and tears and tears because I can't stop,
can't stop, can't stop and I see it all dripping and pool-
ing and souping on Rudi's letter because I can't stop.

I eventually just tip over sideways, onto my bed
again, onto my pillow again, leaving a horrific mess for
whoever comes to claim this spot when I'm gone.

———

The choppers are always so loud. There is no such thing
as a quiet one, and that is probably good. How many
things, really, would you just be better off not hearing
in a war, in any war, in Vietnam?

Parrish and Systrom have come to see me off. They
stand in front of me and I think of how the unit was a
unit when I arrived and now they are two guys who I
don't think even speak to each other much. Headed in

different directions, I figure. Probably for the best. All for the best.

"DERUS, man," Parrish says. "It's just around the corner. Stay strong, Moxie."

We hug, and I just say into his ear, "DERUS," which I think has a nice spiritual sound now. "DERUS," I say. "Maybe we'll start a religion around that."

"It already exists, man," he says, laughing and backing away.

Lt. Systrom steps up, salutes so sharply he could cut diamonds with it. He has gone all the way back to official Armyman now.

And he's wasting no words.

"You are special," he says over the copter roar, which gets louder as it's about to take off. "And you know why you are special."

He finishes off the salute and waves me off into the helicopter. Up.

I look back at the ground, about to wave, and the two of them are chattering as they head back already to the *Benewah*.

I turn and watch the sky road ahead. I crunch my unopened orders in my hand as we lift into the hazy orange sunset.

The pilot knows where we're going anyway.

That makes one of us.

About the Author

Chris Lynch is the author of numerous acclaimed
books for middle-grade and teen readers, including the
Cyberia series and the National Book Award finalist
Inexcusable. He teaches in the Lesley University creative
writing MFA program, and divides his time between
Massachusetts and Scotland.